LA PASSARAN.. ARMISTICE

And Peace They Passed On...

KAUSHIK GHOSH

INDIA • SINGAPORE • MALAYSIA

ISBN 979-8-89067-834-8

Dedicated to Baba…

Song by the German Anti-Nazis in the International Brigade:

Spanish heavens spread their brilliant starlight
High above our trenches in the plain
From the distance, morning comes to greet us,
Calling us to battle once again.

CONTENTS

ABOUT THE AUTHOR

Kaushik's humble beginnings in rural Bengal in the 1980s did not hold him back from achieving academic excellence. From a small village school, he went on to graduate from North Bengal Medical College, pursue post-graduation from Nil Ratan Sircar Medical College in Kolkata, and receive fellowships from prestigious Royal Colleges in England and Ireland. As a medical academician and specialist physician, he has authored numerous publications in the field of medical science.

But Kaushik's interests extend beyond medicine; he is an avid enthusiast of medical history, especially during colonial India. He finds inspiration for his first fictional novel, set during the Spanish Civil War, while writing in medical duty rooms. For Kaushik, the will to fight for life is the best motivator for his creative endeavors.

When not on duty, Kaushik indulges in his passions for travel, attending lectures, and extensive reading. Additionally, he possesses a keen interest in old Hollywood movies and cricket.

ACKNOWLEDGEMENT

I became acquainted with the name Norman Bethune when my father directed my attention to an old map on a glossy paper. Dr. Norman Bethune, a socialist Doctor who embarked on a journey from Canada to China, passing through the battlefields of Spain. In my quest to trace his path, I discovered a few Indian names who volunteered in the Spanish Civil War. Classic Bengali books by Rabin Pal meticulously documents the presence of such individuals on Spanish soil. To pen a fictional novel on this topic was always a cherished dream.

When my father passed away, in my disturbed state of mind I stumbled upon the same old map he had shown. I began the process of writing In fragments. With the assistance of Sharmisthadi, I was able to weave those pieces in the form of this book. Two of my beloved juniors Kalyan and Sonali, consistently inspired me and helped me recognize my potential as a writer.

My daughter Samriddhi, at her tender age of six is the never ending source of encouragement and stamina needed for hours of writing. I am grateful to my beloved wife, Susmita, who's support in my audacious endeavor to write is unwavering.

During the difficult days following the loss of my father, my mother, brother, and nieces served as a constant source of energy. Lastly, I thank Shreedi for all the necessary help.

I must emphasize that this book is not a historical account or a classic tale. Instead, it is a collection of imaginary pieces that have been carefully woven together. My gratitude extends far beyond the names mentioned, specially to all those who were an integral part my journey from childhood into adulthood.

PROLOGUE

The now-familiar sound of the wailing of sirens hit his ears. Henry lay in a hastily dug makeshift trench near Madrid, not daring to breathe. Darkness had descended, but his eyes, over the long months here, had learnt to adjust to the dark. He had cat's eyes but so had the others with him. He could still hear the sound of gunshots afar where fighting raged. The bombers were coming. German Heinkels would soon fly overhead, brandishing their firepower. Flames would erupt. Lives would be lost and there would be work to be done.

He knew every moment he lived could be his last. Now that he was here, there was no way out. The stench of death was all around him. Henry thought if he died just now, it would not be a death of glory. He was not even a soldier fighting for his country. It would be months before anyone at home even knew about his fate. The roar of aircraft engines came to his ears. For the umpteenth time, he thought he did not know what madness had gripped him which had brought him here on foreign soil devastated by civil war, where all he heard was the agonizing cries and all he saw were rubble and debris of what had once been proud buildings.

He had a strange name reflecting his mixed lineage. Although everyone called him Henry, it was not his full name. It was Henry Ravi Jones, given by his fond Indian mother, who had fallen in love with a simple English clerk working in the British Indian government. Soon, his father left India for Britain. He had inherited his father's shock of curly disordered blond hair but had his mother's black eyes. In school, everyone had difficulty remembering Henry's full name. He had simply dropped his middle name. The school was more or less uneventful, interrupted by occasional visits to India to meet his mother's family. It seemed like arriving in a different world – a world which was alien to him. The heat and dust did not bother him as much as some of the comments which dropped on his ears. His mother came from a large family headed by a white-haired patriarch whom he called *Nanaji*. He was always dressed in a khadi kurta pyjama and was an ardent follower of Mahatma Gandhi, the leader of the masses. It was a time when India's struggle for freedom was discussed in every household. Nanaji used to have avid discussions with a group of men in the large courtyard of his house over steaming cups of tea and savoury Indian snacks. His sari-clad *nani*, busy in the kitchen, would wear an irritated frown but did not protest. Henry felt rather like a reluctant stranger forced to eavesdrop on the misdeeds of the British. He was deeply conscious of the fact that his father was a Britisher and that he lived in England.

As he grew up, his time was taken up with English sports and academics. Politics had little to interest him. However, the papers were full of nothing else. Everywhere he went, there was talk. Germany was flexing its muscles again. A new party dubbed as National Socialists or Nazi party headed by a short man with a bottle brush moustache,

Adolf Hitler, had overthrown the chaotic Weimar Republic and captured power. A new aggressive Germany had rearmed itself, throwing the Treaty of Versailles to the winds. Hitler had emerged as the virtual dictator with supreme powers. The German Air Force, Luftwaffe, established as recently as 1935, was already a force to be reckoned with. Hitler found an opportunity to test its might during the Spanish Civil War between the ruling Republicans and usurping Nationalists led by General Fransisco Franco. Hitler and Mussolini of Italy threw their weight in favour of Franco. The Spanish Civil War broke out on 17th July 1936. It attracted massive attention and the world waited with bated breath. The Soviet Union sided with the Republicans. Neville Chamberlain decided on a policy of neutrality. The British felt that another World War had to be avoided at all costs. But in street corners and pubs, the Spanish Civil War was a hot topic for discussion. Willy-nilly, Henry found himself sucked into its vortex. There was talk of nothing else.

One of his close friends, Robert, said, "Our government is weak. It does nothing. I am enlisting tomorrow with the International Brigade. Something has to be done. Hitler must be stopped. The fascists will seize power."

Henry had argued, "But what can we do? It's none of our business."

His friend had said the words which would be imprinted in his mind forever, "Sometimes, the contribution of even one man can make all the difference in the world."

Henry was silent. He found himself accompanying Robert to a cultural meeting organized by Jawaharlal

Nehru's daughter, Indira, to raise funds. What made him go on that fateful day? He did not know the answer. Perhaps, it was curiosity. Slim and sharp-featured, sari-clad Indira Nehru spoke fervently and asked for help. There were other speakers on the stage urging everyone to help in any way they could. Henry found himself being swept in the fervour. At that moment, stopping Franco in any way he could feel was the most pressing need. The madness had begun. Soon, Henry found himself enlisting. He wanted to help the Republicans.

A thin, bespectacled man with a greying moustache who was recruiting asked him, "What is your purpose?"

He blurted out, "To help the sick and the wounded."

The man asked him, "Your name?"

He told him his full name.

The man peered over his spectacles, "Ah, I see you have an Indian connection. Indians support our cause."

He found himself saying, "My mother is an Indian."

The man in the spectacles nodded and then said briskly, his voice more formal, "Do you have any sort of medical training? Have you ever worked in a hospital?"

Henry shook his head in the negative.

The man said, "Don't be disappointed, lad. There is work for all in Spain."

Henry had whispered, "What can I do?"

"You can be a stretcher bearer. You are raw but you will learn as you go along. Norman Bethune is there and he will need all possible help."

This was the first time he had heard the name which would be so familiar in the months to come. Henry's life had changed forever.

CHAPTER 1

Henry lay still in the trench. Soon, there were by now the familiar whistling hissing sounds as the Heinkels and the Junkers unloaded their cargo and scooted away, followed by only weak anti-aircraft fire. Henry covered his ears as the sound of a roar and explosion hit his ears. The sound was disconcertedly near. He peered out and saw the devouring flames hungrily licking everything before it and the all-encompassing clouds of smoke that made your eyes water and crept into your lungs even if you kept your mouth tightly covered. The faint sound of agonizing screams reached his ears. The damage was done. Henry and two others with him got up nimbly. Henry covered his face with a handkerchief left in the pocket of his ill-fitting khaki dusty brown jacket and ran.

Miguel ran alongside him, breathing fast. "That seemed quite near," he said between breaths as they picked up the makeshift stretcher consisting of two wooden poles with a piece of cloth in between that they had discarded when they had dived into the trenches as the sirens wailed.

Holding this contraption which passed as a stretcher, they ran as quickly as possible towards the smoke-filled air, coughing and spluttering. The bombers had gone, but there was darkness everywhere. At times, it was impossible to see where you were treading. The lights, at best, were dimmed. They had to move with care in the undulated terrain lest they fell into shell holes. Many stretcher bearers had been grievously injured and some even lost their lives by taking a wrong step. The cries were growing louder. Henry thought cynically that he still had the capacity to register shock at the sheer destruction, often of innocent lives, although it had become an everyday affair with him. All around him were dead bodies of people taken completely unawares. They lay many of their limbs torn from their body in silence forever. They may be nameless figures now but they were living, breathing beings who were torn asunder by the invaders from the sky. The worst was that many of them had nothing to do with the war. He could see the shapely ankle of a young woman lying underneath a pile of bricks that had once been a wall. The ankle was still clad in a beautiful shoe. Perhaps, thought Henry, the girl had come here to meet her lover. Her lover may be lying dead or would not know her fate. Her parents would worry that their daughter had not returned home. It would be days before they would come to know what had happened to her.

A man was lying on the edge of a pile of debris. He was lying so still, staring with vacant eyes, that Henry thought he was dead. The dead could wait; it's the living who required attention. Instinctively, his hand moved towards the man's pulse. There, he sensed a faint beat.

He turned to Miguel, "There is still a chance. Let's get him out."

They placed him on the stretcher and started running cautiously as it was still dark in the rugged land. The man's eyes suddenly revealed a spark of life. His lips moved.

Henry could hear the word, "Water."

He shook his head.

The man again asked through half-closed eyes, "Is my boy dead?"

Miguel answered candidly. He knew that lying was of no use. "We don't know. Our only job is to carry you to a point. It's like a relay. A medic will attend to you and will send you to a hospital. Other stretcher-bearers will carry you there."

What he did not say was that the medical personnel, not necessarily qualified doctors, would silently categorize the patients. There were too many of them crying for medical attention. There was a sadistic streak in the whole business which could not be helped. Survival of the fittest was the silent rule followed. The medic knew that many of the victims literally lay on their deathbeds on the stretcher in which they were carried. It was not possible to save their lives. They were given cursory attention at the camp and were left to their fate, later to be buried. If there was hope of saving a critically injured victim, especially people of the right age, they were taken to the hospital on a priority basis. This hospital too was set up in haste in the building which once functioned as a school. Other patients who were deemed not so critical were carried to the same hospital, albeit at a slower pace. They were second in the line of treatment.

Henry, at times, pondered whether it was a bit like Nazi Germany, where only the fittest survived. Henry had heard horrific tales coming out from Nazi Germany. It had become a totally autocratic state where no form of dissent was tolerated. Jews were treated like untouchables. They were subjected to immense persecution to the extent that they forfeited their right to live. Everywhere in Germany, they were deprived of basic human and civil rights. The Nazi philosophy was based on the Aryans being the master race and Jews being vermin. The Germans held the Jews responsible for all the ills of the world. One of the first decrees passed by Hitler upon assuming power was excluding Jews from civil services. The Nuremberg Race Laws of 1935 added to their discrimination from all walks of life. They lost their right to be considered for any profession or even business. Their shops were vandalized and gutted. Almost all of them were placed in "Aryan" hands. Many of them were taken away from their homes and put into concentration camps.

Once Henry and Miguel had reached the point, which was a temporary camp, they hurried back to get their next burden. It turned out to be a ragged old man. He was still conscious, though slightly injured. There was an ugly scar on his left arm which had been singed. Fortunately, it was slight.

Though in agony, the man managed to say, "The dammed fascists. Hell with them. They did it to us. I have lived for over sixty years but I have not seen such horror even in the Great War. It's Spain against Spain, brother against brother. Even my neighbour has turned against the government. They worship that traitor, Franco. I have lost my home which I built with all my savings. My boys have all gone to fight. I do not know if I'll see them again."

After a pause, he managed to say looking at the crouched, bent forms, "Where are you taking me?"

Henry had learnt the brevity of words. He simply said, "To help."

The old man said, "Nothing can help me." There seemed to be a tired resignation in his voice.

All Henry managed to say was, "Never give up." The words seemed futile but one never knew how long one has to live.

The next person they picked up was a young teenage boy with a hint of a beard. His trousers were torn and his thigh wounded. Blood was still oozing out where a splinter had hit him. Henry had been trained in first aid but at present, he had nothing with him except a large piece of cloth which could serve as a temporary bandage. Henry had hastily wrapped his thigh with it. The victim's young face was contorted in agony.

He managed to burst out, "It was them bombs." He let out a cry and then continued breathing heavily, "Market place…had to get milk…Bombs…then nothing; just pain and sound of screams." He let out another agonizing scream, "Could not move."

Henry nodded.

The boy asked, "Will I survive? Poor mother. Two elder brothers have gone to the front."

Henry said, "We will do our best. You will soon be in a hospital where a doctor will treat you."

He said with hope in his eyes, "Norman Bethune is in Madrid. Take me to him."

CHAPTER 2

Norman Bethune. Everywhere Henry went he came across the name. Most of them stood in awe of him. Yet, despite his achievements, he remained a controversial figure. To the Republican army, he was regarded as no less than God – a man who brought hope and faith into their lives and like the boy, felt that he was their saviour, a knight in white armour.

One day, while eating dry bread in a rudimentary hut on the Madrid-Valencia Road, Henry asked Miguel, "Have you ever met Norman Bethune? Everyone seems to be talking about him."

Miguel shook his head, "Not personally, but I have heard he is a great surgeon. Perhaps, the greatest surgeon alive."

"Where did he come from?'

Miguel laughed, "Don't you know? Everyone here does. From Canada."

"He worked there?"

"Oh, yes. He did. You know he had already achieved great heights before he came to Spain. He was Chief of Thoracic Surgery at the Sacre Coeur Hospital and a host of other things that I have forgotten."

"Why did he come here?'

Miguel shot back "To save lives, of course. That's his job. I have also heard that he had enrolled himself in the Communist Party of Canada. He has been to Moscow and fervently believed in their philosophy. He is totally against the upstart Hitler and what he represents. Hitler and Mussolini are the ones behind Franco's power. You know that I belong to Italy."

Henry said in a whisper, "Yes."

"I saw through Mussolini but others did not. Maybe, he rode to power because the left had let us down so badly. There was utter chaos when he came to power. Everyone knew he was bent on dictatorship, ruthlessly crushing any dissent. Yet, they worshipped him. He had his skills, of course. Like Hitler, he was a great orator and perhaps had a romantic appeal. He curbed the power of the people. Democracy became a thing of the past. We could foresee that Mussolini would rule forever. I escaped at the first chance I saw. At that time, it seemed the most difficult thing to do – leaving your country and becoming a refugee in another where you do not belong. I went to Switzerland and then joined the International Brigade. I feel a sense of purpose and belonging here. But we are not talking about me but about Norman Bethune."

Another man wearing a blue shirt walked into the hut. It was Gordon, another fellow medic. He was trained and responsible for assisting the doctor on duty. "Excuse me for butting in but I heard a name."

Offering him bread, Henry answered, "We were speaking of Norman Bethune."

Lying down on the rustic hard floor of the hut, Gordon asked, "What do you know about him?"

Henry answered, "Actually, very little."

Munching the piece of bread and resting on one elbow, Gordon said, "Don't you know about his inventions? It was he who invented the rib shears and many other surgical instruments. He is a man dedicated to his work. He gives his cent per cent. Everyone says that he can work for hours and hours. He may not pay attention to others but any patient he attends to will not be disappointed. He listens carefully to all their problems and takes quick action. I have heard that he is swift in performing surgeries. His way is unconventional but effective. What is best in him is his belief in social medicine. He makes no distinction between his rich and poor patients. According to him, all merit attention, the poor more than the rich. He believes that medicine and treatment should be easily accessible to all and free of cost. He brings hope to the poor."

"Have you seen him?"

"Just a glimpse. He was barking orders. Even from a distance, you feel as if you have come across somebody – a man who oozes personal charisma. He is tall and grey-haired with a receding hairline, which is expected for a man of his years. He was dressed like any of us, wearing a blue jacket and trousers. But I've never seen anyone as active and energetic as him. He drives himself to unimagined levels and expects others to do the same."

They could hear the distant sound of the roar of machine gun fire. It was a sound they were familiar with. The wind whistled and there was a chill in the air. Henry rubbed his hands together. It helped him keep warm.

Gordon continued, "In a way, he is like us. Did you know that he actually took part in the Great War as a stretcher bearer in the Field Ambulance Medical Corps?"

Miguel and Henry listened in amazement. "He is a great man indeed, an extremely modest man."

Gordon looked around the rudimentarily furnished hut. The plaster on the walls was falling off. On a shelf that ran around the small one-roomed hut, he could spot a pitcher of water. He carried the pitcher to his lips and gulped down a mouthful.

He laughed, "Far from it. His ego is high – you can expect a man of his achievements to have an ego but I have heard that he is a man who is his own master, unwilling to toe anyone's line. This is all hearsay, of course."

Henry again asked, "Was Dr Bethune born in Canada?"

"Yes. His family is of Scottish origin. I have heard that his father was a small-town clergyman but he preferred to follow in his grandfather's footsteps. His grandfather was a famous doctor. Bethune never wanted to follow his father's profession. He rebelled against it. He is an atheist."

Henry asked, "Then, he was not a doctor in the Great War where he acted as a stretcher bearer?"

"No, no. He studied medicine later. People say there have been many ups and downs in his life. In the Great

War, he was actually wounded by a shrapnel shell in the second battle of Ypres. He then recovered. I have heard that he has had his share of trouble like anyone else in this life. You won't believe it to see him in action but he went down with tuberculosis. There was little hope of him being able to go about his work. Then, he went to a sanatorium in New York. He believed himself dying but he came across a book which saved him."

Henry, his curiosity growing, asked, "Do you know what the book was?"

Gordon nodded, "I have heard about it. It was by Dr John Alexander – *The Surgery of Pulmonary Tuberculosis.* According to it, tuberculosis affecting a single lung could be permanently cured through surgery. The method was new at the sanatorium and he decided to act as a guinea pig himself, fully understanding the risks involved but then, he has always been a calculated gambler. He underwent pneumothorax treatment and it was successful. He was one of the first persons to do so. It pumped new life in him and soon, he was able to resume work."

Henry was staggered. He wondered what kind of unique man Norman Bethune was.

Gordon fished for something in his pocket and then asked in a tired voice, "Can anyone of you lend me a cigarette?"

Henry's hand automatically went to his pocket. He fished out a couple of cigarettes and said ruefully, "Only two left." He offered one to Gordon. He wanted to know more about this remarkable doctor.

Henry remarked, "He seems to be blessed with a lot of innovative skills. He thinks of what others will never do?"

Gordon blew a cloud of smoke which wafted up to the low conical ceiling. He said, "Yes, he is unconventional. Ah, he is a man of many talents. He is an artist as well as a doctor. His fingers have magic in them. Do you know he is an artist with clay, a painter and a great writer? He was all this in one. His mind seemed to be always working even though he was a heavy drinker."

Henry digested this information. Norman Bethune was human after all and suffered from some of their frailties despite the awe-inspiring reputation he had built up. Gordon saw a look of slight shock in Henry's eyes. "Ah, there is a lot you don't know about the man. Don't be shocked. All of us drink. So, why shouldn't a surgeon? He is also an attractive man. Women fall in love with him all the time."

Henry again asked, "Isn't he married?'

Gordon grinned again, "Was. Twice to the same woman, Frances."

"He seems very interesting. I don't know if I'll ever get to meet him."

Gordon murmured, "Don't get disheartened. You may run into him anytime. After all, we are in the same field."

"I am no doc."

"Nor am I, but we do take care of the wounded and sick in whatever way we can."

Gordon's cigarette was over. He stamped out the flickering stub with his feet and then said nonchalantly, "By the way, do you know that Norman Bethune was a poet as well, a fine poet? If you are interested in poetry, I'll try to get some of his poems for you. I must get going."

He moved out, leaving Henry dumbfounded. Was he interested in poetry? His mind was in a whirl. It was their love for poetry that had brought him, Edwina and Robert together. England seemed like a different world altogether with images hard to forget.

CHAPTER 3

Henry and Edwina. Henry had met her at High School at the cusp of a college education. She was the new girl in the class – a girl not striking to look at but not someone you could easily ignore. She had a small face with startling large penetrating grey eyes and a pert nose. Her blond hair was tied in a simple but slightly messy ponytail from which a few tendrils escaped. Dressed simply, she listened to her teachers with rapt attention. Her face wore an animated look. Most boys dubbed her as a nerd and seemed uninterested in her. She too scarcely gave them more than a cursory glance. Robert, Henry's friend, whispered, "Seems a person with airs. Not my type at all. Maybe an introvert totally immersed in herself."

Somehow, Henry found himself defending Edwina although he hardly knew her, "You know, she could be quite friendly. Maybe, she is truly interested in what they are teaching here. I am in poetry. We should not pass judgements when we hardly know her."

Henry took the first opportunity to speak to her. It was recess. He introduced himself, "Hi, I am Henry Jones. We are classmates."

She extended her hand. It was cool to touch. "I am Edwina Morton."

She gazed at him inquisitively, interested to know more but without displaying any vulgar curiosity which his black eyes and different complexion arose. He smiled and said as if in explanation to her glance, "My mother is an Indian."

Edwina sighed, "That's interesting. I enjoy reading about India and its diverse culture. It's a rich land with so much in it. It has great leaders like Mahatma Gandhi. Have you ever met him? You must have visited India many times."

"No, never. My maternal grandfather may have seen him. He lives and breathes politics."

"And you?"

"Not much. At times, I feel guilty for not even reading the newspaper carefully."

Edwina laughed, "I like you. You are frank. I love reading newspapers...anything for that matter. Words interest me. You can read a section about news from India. Gandhi's pictures are always there. It's hard to miss because of his different clothes. He wears just a dhoti. Jawaharlal Nehru is there too. They want freedom."

Henry answered, "Most people want it. All humanity wants to be free but we are all tied up in one way or the other. The desire for freedom from British rule has been there for years. I have been hearing such talk in my grandfather's house since I was a child. All I knew is that they did not like the British and my father was one."

Edwina nodded sympathetically, "Not a nice feeling. Well, I feel independence in India is bound to happen sooner or later. The British will leave, and maybe, Nehru will become the prime minister of a free India. Gandhi is not likely; he does not seem to be interested. I have read that Jawaharlal's daughter Indira is here in London."

Henry asked impulsively, "Are you free in the upcoming weekend? Can we go for a walk?"

Edwina answered, "Oh, yes. I have so few friends here. I enjoy talking to you. Where do you propose to meet?"

"Here, near the gates. Let's explore the countryside. It is great, now that Spring is here."

Edwina smiled. Her face lit up. "Good idea."

It was a balmy Saturday morning when they took a little-known path in the countryside which looked its gorgeous best. A few fluffy white clouds decorated the sky but moved with the wind, throwing them in different paths. The rolling verdant landscape was dressed at its best.

The twisted naked branches of the oaks were once again clothed in vibrant green. Birds chirped and bees hummed. The path they were following twisted through rolling hills, all sporting verdant grass. There were squirrels scampering about and daffodils blooming.

Henry lay down on the grass beneath a shaded oak tree and said to Edwina, "*Hmm*. This is the idyllic countryside. So peaceful. Wish it could last forever."

Edwina smiled, "Unfortunately, nothing does. Things are always changing like the weather. This is reality. We have to enjoy every moment we can."

Henry plucked a blade of grass and chewed its stalk. He felt a delicious juice trickle down his throat. He recited,

"Sweet was the walk along the narrow lane

At noon, the bank and hedgerows, all the way

Shagged with wild pale green tufts of fragrant hay,

Caught by the hawthorns from the loaded wain."

"Wordsworth captures the English countryside very well."

Edwina smiled. Her face was aglow. She spoke softly,

"In the blue of the hills and the blue of the horizon

A mystic hymn with rhyme and rhythm

is being composed in the void and upon the earth.

The gold of the autumn sun bathes the forest.

Violet bees seek honey in the yellow of the flower-bunch.

I am at the centre, therefore

The sky from four sides keeps clapping silently.

Flooded by my joy, today, mingle colours with song."

Henry raised a quizzical eyebrow to which Edwina replied smilingly, "You didn't get that. It's from Rabindranath Tagore. You must have heard of him."

Henry replied, "Who hasn't in India? It is he who first gave the title of Mahatma to Mohandas Gandhi."

Henry laughed, "We have become friends almost like the romantic poets of the era we study. I mean Dorothy and Coleridge. Theirs was a deep friendship – a cauldron of poetry."

Edwina laughed, "Ah, just because we are in the Lake District, you are harping on these romantics. You may fancy yourself a Coleridge but I am no Dorothy. I don't have her temperament, nor do I have a poet as a brother."

Henry kept quiet.

It was a brilliant day. They walked for miles following a trail on the Catbells.

Henry said, "It's not a steep walk. We can make it. I believe the view from the peak has mesmerizing sights of the lakes."

Edwina looked up and said with a glow on her cheeks, "I am game for it."

As they were going, Edwina noticed a few relics. She said, "This is a very old country. It looks like these relics once belonged to my ancestors. Ours is an ancient family. I have heard my grandfather say we can trace our roots back to the Normans."

Henry laughed, "I'm not very sure, but if my father's claims are right, then we are even older. At one time, my remote, remote ancestors were Saxons."

They had reached the top and looked down on the placid lakes, the blue-green waters stretching before them unruffled.

Edwina gasped, "How enchanting."

They stood looking down and then walked back.

Edwina asked, "Have you read Darwin?"

Henry said, "Not exactly but I know that his work, *Origin of the Species*, is under discussion."

"What do you think of it?"

"I think, in a way, he is right. Most people condemn him or think he has committed blasphemy for daring to write what he felt. It is undoubtedly scientific."

"It is banned in our house as we are Catholics. My father would have one of his fits of rage if the book were on our reading list. I was the curious kind and did read it. I can only say that the book is based on logic and reasoning but whether one can agree with it is another question."

On their way back, they stopped at an idyllic farmhouse. Hay was stacked in a corner. Cows grazed. The farmer welcomed them with a wide smile and offered them food consisting of eggs, ham and freshly baked bread along with apple tart with cream.

Edwina gave a smile of satisfaction, "This was delicious. We can't get such fresh food in London."

Their friendship deepened. Robert too joined them. The three of them visited cafes and had ice cream. During the weekend, they often went to the pictures which was the latest rage. Edwina took very little interest in sports. She was not an athletic type. Robert and Henry, however, played cricket and football, which occupied many of their leisure hours. Henry took a keen interest in cricket and followed the test matches played by the English team. Politics was not really his cup of tea at that time.

High School ended. Robert's decision to work as academics had never interested him. Edwina and Henry entered colleges – different colleges. They would meet over the weekend. At the onset of winter, BBC News was the latest craze. Robert and Edwina loved discussing the rapidly changing political situation in Spain.

Edwina would say passionately, "It's not a civil war that is happening in Spain. It's a proxy war between Hitler and Mussolini, supporting Franco's self-styled Nationalists and the Commies backing the Republicans. At present, it is the anti-fascist forces who need our support. Unfortunately, our government is treading the soft path. They refuse to take sides. Neutrality today is the policy of the weak."

"Yes. I was listening to the radio. Franco is victorious but the Republicans are fighting back hard. Hitler has got to be stopped. If he is not stopped sooner than later, he will plunge this world into chaos."

Edwina said, "I feel sad. You must have heard about the Spanish poet, García Lorca."

Robert shook his head.

Edwina said, "I read about him in the library. A good poet and playwright. He belonged to the Generation of 27. He became famous for writing *Romancero Gitano* or what is popularly known as Gypsy Ballads. He had travelled to New York. I wish he remained there but he returned to Spain. He wrote some of his finest plays there. He was close to the great artist Salvador Dalí."

Robert asked, "What happened?"

"He was killed by the Nationalists. I don't know what his fault was. It could be anything. These Nationalists are a cruel lot."

Henry interrupted, "Will you two discuss something else? Wherever I go I only hear of the Spanish war."

Robert grinned. "Well, I'll give you some gossip…" he let his voice trail away.

Henry's ears perked up. He was all attention. "What's the juice?"

"I have finally got your interest. Well, my piece of gossip is of the political sort but it should interest you as it concerns India, a country you are familiar with. You know Jawaharlal Nehru's daughter Indira is here."

"Yes, I do have a certain amount of political awareness. I know she is studying in Oxford."

"Somerville College, to be precise."

Robert continued, his eyes sparkling, "Ah, but you did not know she often makes trips to London. She is going around with a Parsi called Feroz Gandhi. I wonder if they will take the plunge or if will it be too much for even the liberal Nehru to digest."

Edwina added, "It is difficult to predict, but somehow, I feel that Indira Nehru too has an iron will and will get her way if she wants something desperately."

Henry asked, "Is Feroz handsome? I have heard that Indira is beautiful."

Robert answered, "I did come across a photograph of him. He looks rather plump, with flabby cheeks but good-looking in his own way. Well, I have heard that he was once devoted to Indira's mother, Kamala Nehru. That's how they met, I guess."

Henry again asked, "What is Feroz doing here?"

"He, too, is studying at the London School of Economics. He is also associated with India's freedom movement. I read the gossip columns. Indira and Feroz are often seen in an Indian restaurant in the University area. I too feel that Feroz will be the man in her life. They seem very much in love."

Another day, the three of them were strolling in the park. The children were playing happily.

Robert said, "I pity these children. They may grow up just to see bombs dropping on them, a father killed on the front and a mother trying to survive on whatever she can lay her hands on."

Henry said, "Why talk of gloom and doom? There may not be a war involving England. Hitler is not that mad. The sun has come out. So, let's enjoy."

Robert pointed out, "It's a weak sun. It may go away soon. Chamberlain is trying his best to ward off war but he too may not succeed. A policy of appeasement never pays."

Edwina said, "War is next door to Spain. Everyone here condemns the Fascists but very few do something about it. I hear they are recruiting for the International Brigades for the Republican cause. If the likes of Hitler and Franco are defeated now, the world will breathe better."

This was the first time Henry heard about the International Brigades. He found himself asking Edwina, "Where are they recruiting?"

"I think right here in London. I could have gone had I been a man but my parents are very conservative. Anyway, my heart is in academics. I enjoy English Literature. Someday, maybe I can help people in some way. I have yet to think of one."

The sun had gone out and a chilly wind blew.

Henry shivered. "Let's go back. It's not pleasant here anymore."

They came across a poster.

Edwina said enthusiastically, "Read it. This is so interesting. I have heard that both Jawaharlal Nehru and Indira are espousing the cause of the Spanish Republic. They are collecting funds. Indira is also seeking volunteers for the International Brigade. We must go."

Henry frowned, reading the poster carefully. "It's a fundraising event and my pocket is empty. What will I do?"

Robert suggested, "Oh, come on, Henry, be a sport. You, with your Indian connection, should be more eager than anyone else to go. If nothing, we will expand our knowledge and we will have a pleasant evening. Shanta Gandhi's dances, I have heard, are class. Then, there is Mira Devi's classical Indian dance as well as Spanish ones. You don't have to dole out anything to simply go to the event."

Edwina said, the eagerness in her voice hard to miss, "Yes, let's go. It will give us an opportunity to see Indira Nehru. I love dances, both Indian and Spanish. Do say yes, Henry."

Carried away by the enthusiasm of his friends, Henry agreed. His fate was sealed. It was an evening like no other. It drugged their mind. Decisions were made.

Robert had enlisted as a soldier. He left a day before Henry waving enthusiastically. "I will kill them damned fascists and come back. We will meet here again and have larks."

Henry gave him a warm tight hug and then left.

Soon, it was time for his departure as well. Edwina came to bid farewell at the train station. It was crowded. Henry watched Edwina. A few tears trickled down her eyes though she smiled and tried to check them.

Henry said, "Come on, Edwina. I am not even going to fight. I'll come back whole."

Edwina nodded but could not speak. Henry wondered if Edwina felt more than friendship for him. Did she care more for Robert? He never knew. This is one of the reasons he never tried to take their relationship to another level. It was difficult to know where one stood with Edwina. There was an inner core of reserve which was hard to penetrate. There were things she kept to herself.

After boarding the train, Henry felt a choking sensation. He gulped it down at once. He had a feeling that he would not return to his old life ever again. In this feeling he was right.

CHAPTER 4

Henry came back to the present with a startling cry from Miguel. "Henry, stop daydreaming. There is work to be done."

Henry could not help muttering, "Not a moment to stand and stare."

Miguel said, giving him a slight push, "You've gone daft. Come on, pick up the stretcher.'

Henry shook his head, "Yes. Coming. That's why we are here."

Henry and Miguel were a part of the medical team of the Saklatvala Battalion. It was also known as the British Battalion. The International Brigades consisted of a motley of such battalions, including the Abraham Lincoln Battalion, Naftali Botwin Battalion, Thälmann Battalion, the Garibaldi Battalion, the André Marty Battalion, etc. There were hardly any Spaniards in these Brigades. These International Brigades were made up of foreigners who had joined voluntarily, believing in the Spanish cause. Robert must be in one of them. When Henry first came to Spain, his eyes searched for Robert. He longed to see the familiar face and hear his hoot of laughter in the strange surroundings. But he had not found him. He must be in some other Battalion fighting in the front. A few days after he was given what he felt was rudimentary training in a makeshift barrack, he was put to work like the others of his batch. There had been no time to search.

They had many intellectuals and celebrities in these battalions. As Miguel was fond of saying, "We are in elite company. There is no dearth of celebrities and writers. Half of the world's journalists are here. Some of them have even taken up guns."

Henry replied, "Most of them are Soviet guns."

Wherever they went, they could see traces of Soviet-made weapons and posters displaying the communist's sickle and hammer. The people, too, seemed influenced by it. A peasant whom Henry met on the wayside said, "It's the Russians who are helping us. We are turning into Commies. There is very little difference between the rich and the poor. The war has made everyone poor."

What he said was true. The only countries which actively came to the aid of what was the legitimate democratically elected government of Spain were the USSR and Mexico. Everyone else, including Britain, France and the United States, were neutral.

Dressed in corduroy breeches and a shirt which had seen better days, the man said, "You look like a foreigner."

"Yes, British. I work for the International Brigade."

"This place is crawling with foreigners. They want to help the Republicans. But there is a shortage of arms. Those with Franco have them."

"Yes, German and Italians."

The raw-faced, tanned peasant shook his head and then said, "I wish this war comes to an end soon. It's all very well to feel we are fighting for a cause but war is a total waste of men and land. My fields which were once green are barren. The earth is black and brown, scarred beyond recognition. There are deep holes and shells lying everywhere. My plough is a patchwork. It has been broken several times. It hardly does its job. Almost every able-bodied man is away fighting for what they believe to be the cause. They have never picked up a gun in their lives. A few days of training does not make you a soldier. They don't know anything, just that they will fight with odd romantic notions in their heads. What can they do except hope to kill a few odd fascists? Sometimes, I feel there is nothing to be proud of in a war. It's destructive. The women suffer. Mothers, sisters and daughters. Children become orphans. In the village, they can barely survive, having a hard time trying to make the little they have to go a long way. Mothers often don't eat, hoping their children do."

Henry nodded, touched. The peasant had painted a true picture. His eyes clouded for a moment then he was his usual self. "Goodbye. I'll have to hurry."

It was a bright clear day. The sun was there but was marred by clouds of smoke where shells had hit. Madrid would not see a clear day for a long time. The terrain was rocky in places.

Henry and Miguel reached the camp where the doc on duty said, "No time to lose. Get about your work. These brave boys need to be got to a hospital at once."

Henry answered almost in a robotic fashion, "Yes." He looked up with startled eyes. The doctor had an Indian face. The doctor, too, noticed Henry staring at his brown unshaven face with large black eyes and thin lips. It was a handsome face which was startling because it was Indian.

Henry quickly gathered his wits about him. He could not help asking, "Are you from India?"

The man smiled, "I can see why you are interested." He extended his hand, "I am Dr Madan Mohan Lal Atal. Yes, I am from India. You must have heard about the great Indian National Congress leader Jawaharlal Nehru. He is a staunch anti-Fascist and a supporter of the Republican Cause. Inspired by him, I joined the Spanish Medical Aid Committee. So, here I am. I try my best to treat as many patients as I can in whichever hospital I am posted but it is not even one per cent of what Norman Bethune is doing."

Henry stared at him in awe, "You know Norman Bethune?"

"Yes, I had the honour of working with him. He is nothing short of a genius. He has his ways, but they are successful. Look at his mobile blood transmission unit. It is his innovative ideas that have saved the lives of countless soldiers. He often does it himself. I have seen him at work. He drives himself hard and expects others to do the same. With him, the patient comes first. He handles them with a feeling of tenderness, although he is not exactly tender. As a surgeon, he is easily the best I have seen. He is especially suited to wartime, where every minute requires innovation. He is a man of quick thinking and quicker action. He can perform surgery for hours, improvising and making do with whatever resources are available. Hospitals, too, are in a sad state. We run out of supplies fast. Supply cannot even meet one-third of the demand. The best part is that Bethune treats the poor with the same compassion and attention if not more than the rich, which is a rarity these days – a true commie. Mind you, he has a quick temper but fortunately, I have never been at the receiving end. I have never seen a person like him."

Henry was listening with rapt attention to the narrative. A bullet whistled by and struck a tree as they ducked. Another followed in quick succession. They both dropped to the ground and lay flat against the earth.

Atal shouted, "They have begun fighting again. Hurry up and go to the trenches in the front. Now, run as fast as your legs can carry you."

Henry and Miguel rushed out. The front was out in the hills around two miles away. They ran up the hilly slopes pockmarked with shells and loose earth, which exposed the rocky interior removing the green covering completely. With hearts pounding and adrenaline coursing through their veins, Henry and Miguel rushed out of their hiding spot. The front, where the battle raged on, lay in the distance, nestled among the rolling hills that stretched out for miles. Determination fuelled their every step as they sprinted up the hilly slopes, each one pockmarked with the remnants of shells and loose earth. With each footfall, the ground shifted beneath them, exposing the rocky interior and stripping away the once vibrant green covering that had adorned the landscape.

Henry slipped once and Miguel shouted, "Watch your step. You'll break your neck if you are not careful. There is a ravine by the side."

Henry cast a quick glance. What Miguel said was true. It sent a shudder down his spine. Just on the side of the hill they were climbing was a steep rocky ravine. One misstep and you could plunge to sure death.

As they were climbing to the Republican position, a shell burst near them, sending a cloud of black smoke into the air. Henry tried to shelter his mouth and nose with the help of his elbow, muttering, "That was close."

His mouth was full of dust, and some had also entered his lungs. If only there was a drink or even a glass of water, it would bring relief. But such luxuries were now a far cry, especially in what they called 'action.' The air was filled with the acrid smell of explosives bursting nearby. Henry reflected that more men died of bad air and sickness than bullet wounds. Coughing and spluttering, they headed for the Republican position. The smell of excrement and wasted food assailed Henry's nostrils. A fluttering red flag and screams of "*Fascistas mariconas*" rent the air. They had reached. It was hardly a military position. There were just a couple of trenches, a few sandbags thrown hurriedly to protect the gunners taking positions and the still remnants of the smoke of burnt-out fires. As they approached, the smell of excrement grew stronger. The trenches were littered with them as well as tins and bread crusts. The action did not happen continuously. There were long pauses. On the opposite hill, Henry could perceive a machine gun nest and the Nationalists' flag fluttering, letting off a volley or two. As he entered the trench to pick up the wounded, his eyes scanned the people, automatically looking for Robert. There was no one remotely like him. Most men were stinking. They had not taken a bath for months. Water was scarce and used only for drinking. There was a stream not too far off although you had to trudge miles to get there and its water was icy cold. A dip in its freezing waters could kill you. The trousers and shirts of the men had a worn look. Perhaps, they did not have any change of clothes. Time hung heavily in their hands. They had little to do but wait. Stationary warfare was boring. From here, the enemy was simply black dots who fired sporadically. Sometimes, they found their mark and a cry of agony could be heard. There was a retaliatory fire. Henry once again thought as he caught a soldier stifling a yawn that life for real-life soldiers could be a dead bore – sometimes, even as dull and wearisome as a city clerk. However, there was one very different factor. The life of a city clerk was predictable. One day followed another with very little change. There was very little discomfort. You woke up in your own bed. Here, however, life was unpredictable. Life itself was a big gamble. One could lose it anytime or be maimed for life. Hunger and discomfort were a part of your daily life.

The moment they jumped into the trench, a soldier said, irritated, "You all took your time coming. My comrade here needs immediate treatment. He got the bullet in his thigh and the bleeding has not stopped. Take him to Norman Bethune. He will know what to do."

Henry did not tell him that this was not in his power. He was just a stretcher bearer. He had no decisive power. He did not tell that he had never come face to face with

Norman Bethune. Today, he had the first aid kit with him. He tried to pacify the cries of the soldier by applying first aid and talking to him soothingly.

As they were carrying the soldier, he spoke in stucco bursts, "I hope the docs fix it. Pain unbearable. Bullet got me from machine guns." He again let out an agonising scream and then lost consciousness. Henry deposited the soldier to the nearest camp, hoping that he would pull through and went quickly back to pick up the next victim. He looked up. From here, it was possible to spot the giant snow-clad Pyrenees, which towered over Spain, watching its fate without being affected.

That day, Henry and Miguel made many trips. Some of the men he rescued were teenage boys who were not sure why they were there.

One of them, who was ill, said, "We are basically peasants working in the fields. One day some important officials came to our home. They knocked at our door and said, 'We need people to fight for the government. People all over the world have come to help us on their own. Everyone is taking up arms to help save democracy. We will create a new world order.'"

"It sounded great to me. I felt that I, a poor peasant, was needed and had an important role to play in saving democracy and the world. At that time, I thought going to battle was fun. You just kill a few rebels who are creating trouble and then come back to your village as a hero and maybe get a government job. But that did not happen. I did not know that the war was so disgusting. It makes an animal out of you, no matter which side you are on. Then, the disease kills you. It's this fever."

It was a long day for Henry. One of the men in the trenches complained to him, "We live like pigs here. No hygiene. Nights are dark and cold. Half our time is spent gathering firewood. These hills are of no use. They are almost barren and the vegetation here takes a long time to light up. I can tell from here that the enemy is in no better shape. They, too, are facing difficulty. I can't help feeling a bit for them. They are, after all, poor misguided human beings who have been seduced by Franco into making this war. We are short of food and ammo. It takes time for supplies to get here. Our orders are not to abandon our position at all costs, or the enemy will take over. So here we are, sticking around day in and day out with many of our fellows dying – some of wounds and some of sickness. The enemy has not advanced either. So far, we have held them off. Sometimes, I can't help thinking if it is worth it."

The sun was now gone and black clouds covered the sky. Running to and fro in the hills had tired Henry. Miguel was dispatched to a different errand. Now, he had a different partner to help carry his burdens. He looked up at the sky and shivered. He simply hoped it would not rain. He was too tired. His legs felt like they would buckle under him. All he wanted to do was to find a quiet place and go to sleep.

The clouds burst and the sky was lit not by flashes of explosives but by nature flashing its armoury of thunder and lightning. Henry looked around. His partner had disappeared. Soon, huge drops of rain fell on the earth. Henry was drenched to the skin. His wet shirt was plastered to his body. The road, which was a dirt track, was now slushy. Everything turned into a morass of mud, the stunted bushes growing in the hills failing to protect the earth. Wading through this muddy morass made progress achingly slow. The mud got into his boots and insects crawled on his legs, pin-pricking him with their bites. Henry was forced to drag his feet one after another, taking care. However, he felt so weary that all he wanted was to lie down and sleep. His legs ached so much that he felt he could not go a step further, let alone attend to anyone. He felt a deadness creep into his brain. His head was whirling and every part of his body seemed to ache. Perhaps, he had done too much. His legs wanted to collapse but he could not allow them to. He had to go on. The track was very slippery. It was too dark to see anything except when the landscape was lit by flashes of lightning. On the other side was the ravine. One false step and down he would go. He had to reach for help. The rain continued to beat upon his body in its merciless lashing. There was no respite. He shivered feeling very cold, his plastered shirt hardly giving him any protection. He longed for a warm bed and blanket as his teeth chattered and his limbs seemed to slowly freeze. The whirling and buzzing in his ears increased. He felt going even a step further would require a herculean effort, which he was incapable of. His heart seemed to be leaping from his body. It was running so fast. His limbs were slowly going out of action. A numbness crept into them, which he could not shake off. There seemed nothing he could do. Henry lay down and then, he felt blissful oblivion.

CHAPTER 5

Henry could feel he was lying on a bed with a pillow underneath his head. He opened his eyes and stared at his strange surroundings. This was not a hospital bed. He was inside a house with painted walls. A picture hung on one of them. It looked like a painting – a pastoral scene.

It was a small room painted in sombre tones of cream, but everything was kept neatly. The bedsheet smelled freshly washed and he was covered with a blanket which, though old, was solid and felt warm. He was dressed in pyjamas and a simple oversized shirt which obviously did not belong to him. He wondered how he had got here. All he remembered was feeling exhausted and a feeling of utter helplessness – a feeling he would die and that it was better to give up instead of fighting back and letting the darkness envelop him. The image of lashing rain and wading in almost knee-deep mud came to him. But then, the memories faded. He did not know how he got here and who had looked after him. He tried to raise himself on his elbow but fell back again, his head whirling.

A voice from the doorway said, "I wouldn't if I were you." It was a soft feminine voice – a voice he did not know.

He uttered the first thing that came to his mind, "Who are you? Where am I?"

The woman advanced into the room. She had a graceful walk. Henry looked up at her face and was struck. Emerald-green eyes looked down at him with concern. She had a small forehead with what almost seemed like a perfectly sculpted nose, high cheekbones and full rosy lips which curved in a hesitant smile. What struck him were her bright red curls piled on top of her head.

"*Hola.* I am Rosa. You have been very sick. Perhaps that's why you don't remember. We tried watching over you. At last, the fever has broken."

Henry asked again, a puzzled frown on his forehead, "How did I come here? This seems to be a private house."

Rosa answered again in a soft voice of hers, "*Papa* brought you here. He found you lying unconscious on the hillside. He dragged you here and since then, you have been here. This is our home."

Henry gave a weak smile. He tried to get up once again but failed. Rosa said, "You are still weak. It will take time before you are up and about."

"I am in a village?"

"Yes, in the outskirts of a village quite near Madrid. It cannot be termed exactly a village. It was just a cluster of houses, a bit isolated. I live here with my father and brother."

Henry muttered, "Are these your father's clothes I am wearing?"

"Yes. Though I agree they are too big for you. We had little choice. We were forced to throw away the clothes you were wearing. They were rotten. They wouldn't even stand a wash. Now, rest. You should not speak too much. It will tire you. I will get you a bowl of soup."

It was much later that Henry managed to swallow a few spoonfuls of soup with chunks of meat floating on it which Rosa fed him slowly. As the soup trickled down his throat – a warmth spread all through his body.

He managed to say, "*Gracias.* It's the best soup I have tasted for months."

Rosa smiled, "It's homemade from sheep. I guess it's a long time since you last tasted food at home."

Henry closed his eyes. His mother was a superb cook. She could make both Indian and Continental food. He remembered her lip-smacking lentil soups which they called dal, assorted vegetables, baked bread which they called roti and of course, rice which were a part of his food until he left home beside the usual lamb, chicken, fish, bacon and eggs. Henry's mother remained a practising Hindu and refused to have beef. She encouraged her children to desist, but they suffered no such scruples. Cows were worshipped as sacred animals in India. There was a small room which he called the prayer room in his home. It had idols of various Gods and Goddesses. His mother would sit on the floor and pray. As a child, Henry was not interested in prayers but looked forward to the sound of the tinkling of bells. On hearing the sound, he would run to the prayer room. There, his mother would offer him specially made sweetmeats which she had prepared as *Prasad* or offering to God.

The soup went down into his belly and he slept again. When he woke up, there was no Rosa but a man of middling years with a shock of grey and white hair. He was much taller than Henry, with broad, powerful arms and shoulders and a wide forehead.

He asked, "Have I been very sick?"

The man answered, "*Si*. You have been wracked by fever which lasted three days. You were unconscious most of the time. By the way, I am Jose, a small farmer. What's yours?"

Henry managed to extend his arm and said, "Henry."

Jose again asked, "You are a soldier in the army? When you were in a delirium, you talked of battles, bombing, the sick and the wounded."

"Nothing so glamorous. I am a stretcher bearer. I was separated from my companion when the rains came. Maybe, I got lost. I don't know. All I remember is the rain and slush, the shivering cold and the utter weariness that gripped me. I felt I could not go a step further. I must have fainted away. I was lucky that you found me. I would have been a dead man by now."

Jose scratched the side of his cheek, which revealed a grey stubble and said, "Maybe, but it's all a matter of chance. Maybe, God willed it so. We are devout Catholics. We try to go to church every Sunday. It is not possible every week now with the war and uncertainties. I know that most Catholics are behind the Nationalists but we favour the Republican Cause. It is a democratically elected government. I had gone out to get some bushes from the hillside. I had gone far when it started to rain. I was caught. So, I hurried back when I saw you lying there. At first, I thought you were dead. You were so still; no movement at all. I put my hand under your nose. I could feel your breath. I ran my hand on your face. Your entire body was on fire. Your clothes were muddy. I did try to wake you by shaking you, but that did not work. I tried to lift you and throw you over my shoulder, but it was difficult, so I dragged you to a point. Then, I met people I knew and hailed them. They helped me bring you home. I live here with my daughter and son. A local doctor has seen you. He gave us a few medicines which brought your fever down. My son has gone out but Rosa must be bustling up some food for you."

Henry stammered, "Thank you so much for everything. I know I owe my life to you."

The man airily waved his hand, "Oh! It's God you have to thank, not us."

Rosa came in with freshly baked bread and Patatas Bravas. "Potatoes constitute a major chunk of what we eat. This is Spanish food."

She had changed her dress. She was wearing a red ankle-length skirt which she paired with a white blouse. Some of her hair had escaped the bun and she brushed it aside with her left shoulder. She placed the food on the side table and later, placed her arm on his shoulder to help raise him, saying, "Take it easy."

Her hands felt soft even though they were a working woman's hands. He ate quietly and said, "Thank you."

Rosa smiled, "Did you like the food?"

Henry said, "It's the best food I've had for a long time."

Rosa asked again, "I have heard that you are fighting for the Republicans?"

"Not exactly fighting, helping them out. I am working as a stretcher bearer although I am not fit for anything now. I can't even move."

Rosa smiled and in an encouraging voice, said, "You will be able to in a couple of days. Nothing is, you know, permanent."

Nothing, you know, is permanent. Henry would remember these words later.

CHAPTER 6

He woke the next morning feeling better. Of course, he was in Rosa's house. He had come to think of it as Rosa's house. Henry sat up on the bed and found he could do so without falling back. He gingerly stepped down and stood up after rolling up the pyjamas so that he would not trip. He was still unsteady, but at least he could take small steps without help, even if they were tottering steps. That morning, when Rosa came with his breakfast – a thin porridge along with fresh eggs – she introduced him to her brother, Albert. Albert was large like his father with brown hair and blue eyes.

He said, "Good to see you better. When Dad brought you here, we did not see any hope. You were almost gone..."

Rosa interrupted him, "Must we talk about it? It's not pleasant. He is just beginning to recover."

Albert scowled at his sister, muttering, "I didn't mean any harm. I just thought he should get the picture right."

Henry said, "I am very grateful for what you all have done for me. I realise that I could have been dead."

Albert said in an embarrassed voice, "Glad to be of help. No need to worry; you'll pull through."

Albert sat beside his bed and asked, "What was it like, the war?"

"Horrifying. I didn't fight though."

Albert said, "Then, I am glad I didn't jump in. Almost every able-bodied man in the nearby villages joined up. They went away with great enthusiasm singing patriotic songs. Everyone here expected me to do so. I stayed back. Most people did not like it. They looked at me as if I had done something wrong but I didn't care. Dad is not in great shape. I can't leave Rosa alone, either. He needs looking after. Then, there is our small farm. It is a small holding. What we have got is through difficulty. We are not rich and never will be like the grandees but we do have the satisfaction of making two ends meet. At least in these hard times, we can eat even if we live simply without any luxuries. We are better off than many who are starving half their days."

Henry said, "You did the right thing. There should be someone to till the land. Otherwise, there will be no food."

Albert nodded, "There is already scarcity. Much of the land is lying barren. Food is scarce. I have heard that life is hell in Madrid. There is a shortage of almost everything, including matchsticks, gas, potatoes, coal and fuel. People are queuing up to buy a loaf of bread. Here, we are better off because of our farm and the few livestock we have. The air is relatively clean."

"Yes. Everything is important in a war, even those who serve their home. But I hope it ends soon."

"I hope so too, or Spain will be completely destroyed. Not that it was in great shape earlier. Politically, we were very unstable. Governments came and went. There were always revolts. Military dictatorship came. Although it brought a bit of order, the lives of people were subdued. The monarchists were equally bad. I can't say we enjoyed political freedom, but at least the bloodshed was comparatively low. Franco's sudden rise to power is not new. Spain has always been under the thumb of the military. It is they who call the shots. The elected governments were under their thumb. The church also has power. They control the education." He paused for breath. Then said, "By the way, where did you come from? You are obviously not Spanish. How did you get entangled in our war?"

"I joined the International Brigade like countless others."

"Yes, I see. Spain is crawling with foreigners. I have heard that all the hotels are full. There are also many people from well-to-do families who have joined the Republicans. But still, I do not have a gut feeling that we will win."

Henry said, "I know Franco is powerful. He has a united army, which has experience in Africa. The best in Spain, I believe. What is more to the point is that he is backed by Hitler and Mussolini who have powerful armies. Hitler's military power is on the rise and Spain is serving as a testing ground. They may have the arms but Republicans have the manpower and spirit. Why even if our governments don't, people all over the world support the Republican cause. They have volunteered to fight for democracy and freedom – all that which Franco negates. I agree that Republicans are a divided lot with very little organization. They do not present a united front. The International Brigade has volunteers from almost 60 countries. However, most of them fight almost with the same zeal as a Spaniard."

By the next day, Henry felt his strength was slowly returning. He waited eagerly to hear the sound of Rosa's footsteps and the rustle of her skirt. He could not help thinking about her startling emerald eyes with eyelashes that curled upwards, the arch of her throat when she looked up, and her lips which curved while smiling giving an additional glow to her face. Henry's eyes were fixed on the doorway. Rosa entered with the food tray.

Henry said, "I can help myself now. Thanks for the food. I hope I am not wasting your time."

Rosa smiled, "I like talking to you. We have so few visitors here."

Henry's smile broadened. "You cook very well."

Rosa smiled broadly, "*Gracias.* Not as well as your mother."

"Yes, but home is a long way off. I don't know when I will be able to return home."

Rosa hesitated and then said, making an effort, "I don't know how to say this. I am expressing myself badly. In the delirium, you spoke of a woman called Edwina. I think you must have left a lot behind."

Henry flushed and then said, "Edwina is a friend in England. We studied together in High School and have been friends since then."

Rosa smiled, "Forgive my feminine curiosity. I thought she was your sweetheart."

Henry smiled ruefully, "No such luck. We were just friends. I have left no sweetheart back home. That is one thing I do not regret."

Henry wondered why Rosa was asking this question.

Rosa said, "What made you join up? This is, after all, not your country."

Henry explained, "It was in the atmosphere. Everyone in England would talk only of Spain and politics. My friends Edwina and Robert were totally into it." He began his story.

Rosa listened with rapt attention. Rosa let out a deep sigh, "You gave up a lot. Your education, things you loved, your family and a whole way of life to fight for our country."

Henry said simply, "At that time, it seemed to be the most important thing in the world."

"How did you feel once you got here?"

"In the beginning, euphoric though getting into Spain from England was difficult. It's a long story. On the train, everyone seemed to hoot for us. Almost all were discussing Spain, sitting on the rough wooden benches of the compartments. We were given a hero's welcome at the station, although we had done nothing. People seemed to feel that just by coming here, we had done something great, which, of course, we did not do. People alighting from the train were a strange bunch of people. We belonged to all races and all possible nationalities. At the station, you could see men and even a few women of all skin colours – black, brown, Asian and, of course, white. It was as if they had arrived to participate in games."

Rosa asked, "Were you trained?"

Henry gave a sad smile, "Semblance of it. Just basic first aid. There was a shortage of time. We were kept in a barracks along with soldiers who would be given training almost without firearms. Most of them were raw too, new kids willing to lay down their lives for a cause. But they had to be taught how to fire and load the rifle. There were very few rifles in the barracks which could be used to train. Sometimes, this was all the training they received, just learning to fire shots if they were lucky enough to get hold of a rifle and strut about in a parade. This was of very little use to a soldier. They were not taught the tactics of warfare like running for cover, preparing barricades, tackling the enemy, running in the open ground, capturing the next military point, etc."

"A different life altogether from the one you had at home. It must not have been comfortable in any way."

Henry could not help laughing, "That's the understatement of the year. The barracks were cramped with almost a thousand men at a time and the few women who did the cooking and other chores. We were woken up by a quivering kind of Spanish bugle call. Even the bugle callers were amateurs like all of us. The place reeked of horse shit though most of the horses had left for the front, carrying supplies and men. There were a few moments of fun as well. We were encouraged to play to build a team spirit. So, we played football with almost fifty in a team. We were made to undergo long parades early in the morning, though we were not training to be soldiers. However, physical fitness was important for even us stretcher-bearers. I remember the chomp, chomp of hobnailed boots in the backyards of our barracks."

Rosa sighed, "Very hard."

Henry burst out, "The life that followed was harder. There was hardly any time to eat and sleep. The scenes which we came across were too agonizing to be described to a woman."

Rosa almost smiled, but she quickly assumed a grave countenance. "Women are tougher than what most people think. They go through a lot but may not always express themselves. You, too, have suffered."

Henry said shortly, "Well, perhaps not as much as soldiers in the front or even women suffering silently at home. Come on, let's not talk about it. What I am now experiencing is nothing short of heaven for me – a warm bed to lie in and delicious food served to me every day by a beautiful woman. There is nothing more any man can desire."

Colour flooded Rosa's cheeks. She muttered, her eyelashes downcast, "You are too kind. I don't deserve any such praise."

Henry felt he had embarrassed her. He tried to change the topic. "When I am slightly better, I would like to see the farm."

The next day, Henry felt he was improving. He was able to accompany Rosa on a short tour of the farm. Now that

Henry felt strength returning, he was able to see that this was a typical village hut made of stone and plaster around a small farm. It was a bright crisp day. The battle seemed far off as no sound of gunfire or bursting artillery shells reached his ears. There was an eerie silence broken only by their chatter and mooing of cows and the cackling of hens. The rolling grassland around them was green and the olive trees lining the farmland seemed to sway in the gentle breeze. There was a limited kitchen garden where Henry could spot spring onions, white and plump.

Henry sighed. The farm had brought memories back of Edwina and his day spent in the countryside. He said, "This is like a way of life which is fast disappearing because of the war."

Rosa said, "Yes, it's a pity. Sometimes, I feel that our house is like an oasis, still clinging to a bit of the past. Everything else is changing so quickly, even the landscape. Once, Spain was known for its culture, now it is known for war."

Henry said, "I have heard about the famed bullfights."

Rosa was reminiscing, "You know, Alfred wanted to become a matador. But my father was against it. He said that even with training, the fate of a matador is uncertain. It is not always that a man wins. Sometimes, nature wins as well. So, Alfred's dream was not realized."

Rosa asked, "What was your dream?'

Henry laughed, "Those days seem so far off now. A time to dream. I wanted to become a teacher of literature. I am fond of reading and poetry."

"You can go back to your old life once you leave. After all, you are a volunteer."

Henry said passionately, "No. That's not possible. My conscience will not allow it. Strangely enough, now I believe in the cause. I will go back the moment I feel better. I don't know if I am playing an important role in the war. I am not a glorified commander, just a stretcher bearer. I am not exactly qualified for anything else."

Rosa turned indignant green eyes towards him, "Why do you call yourself *just* a stretcher bearer? It's one of the best services one can render. You are the first to reach those who need help. It's your hands that pick them up and carry them to safety. The very sight of you brings hope to the eyes of those who are dying. Without our stretcher bearers, where will we be? Never ever think that what you are doing is a lesser contribution than anyone else."

Rosa had tied her hair into a loose bun. It became undone and fell down her back. The sun's rays glittered on it, making it look like molten gold against her simple white printed dress. Henry's heart skipped a beat. He had never seen anything so enchanting. He felt a strange longing – a longing to run his fingers through her hair. He gave himself a shake. What was he doing? He could not be caught staring at her as if he had never seen a woman before.

He spoke the first thing that came to his mind. "Talking of help, have you heard of Norman Bethune?"

Rosa had gathered her hair and was about to tie it into a bun when she stopped, her fingers still intertwined in her hair. "I seem to have heard the name. He is a doc, isn't he?

Many of the people I have met speak of him with reverence. Have you met him?"

Henry shook his head sadly, "No. I have never had that honour. I wish I could someday. However, I have come across an Indian doctor who has worked closely with him. He feels that Norman Bethune is a man who is one in a thousand. Everyone I have met also talks about him with a kind of awe. Besides, his personality is such that he commands respect. Not only medical personnel but wounded soldiers and civilians have tremendous faith in him. They feel all they need to do is to reach Dr Bethune."

Rosa had finished tying her bun, "There are many times when I too feel that I am not doing anything really fruitful by staying home. The war has torn people's lives asunder. Almost every family has suffered. Everywhere, people are crying for help. I still feel at times that I could have become a nurse or taken on any other woman's work like sewing clothes."

Henry said, "Don't fret. You are doing a great job where you are. I am a living example. Your food and care have made me stand on my feet again."

Rosa burst out laughing. It was a full-throated laughter which sent a tingling sensation down Henry's spine. He wanted to hear the laughter again.

He said, "Some credit should go to the livestock here, the cows who give milk, the fowl meat and eggs.'

She laughed again.

He turned again and said in a more serious voice, "Now that I can move about, I should be going back."

Rosa said, "You could stay a few days more." He could not make out from her tone whether she said it out of sympathy, a feeling of friendship or a genuine desire for his companionship.

"I am afraid that it is not possible. I have to go back."

Rosa said, "Then, we will be losing you soon."

CHAPTER 7

Jose sat beside Henry outside the house. The tall ancient trees that surrounded them told no tales of blood and horror.

Jose sighed, "You will go away soon and I will miss you. I am afraid sometimes you may find my gab boring, but then I have so few with whom I can share my thoughts."

Henry said, "Not at all. I can never repay what you have done for me. Without your timely help, I would have been a dead man."

Jose said simply, "I would have done the same to any other man; it was my duty. In Spain, you learn to live with death."

'Yes. It's the Civil War. Hitler's rise in Germany is alarming. Look at the way he is treating Jews. They are being driven out in fear of their lives."

"Yes, but antisemitism is not new. It was there in Spain too. I think it is a part of European culture. In Spain, too, Jews suffered. We have a long and chequered history of barbarity. But I hope that I am not boring you. My tales are rather long."

"Please go on. I am very interested in the history of your country," said Henry.

Jose needed no more encouragement. "Our history goes back a long time. This part of the land was then known as part of the Iberian Peninsula. Perhaps, once the early man stage was crossed, people led a nomadic life. Then, they reared sheep and captured grazing land. Later city-states were set up. Then the Romans came and we were a part of the Roman Empire. Perhaps this was the beginning of civilization, as we understand it in the modern sense. Then, the Christians came and later Muslims. The peninsula flourished under the Muslims, especially its art and culture. Later the Christians reconquered Spain. Therefore, the Spain that emerged in the medieval era was a melting pot of different religions and cultures, which included Jews, Muslims and Christians."

Henry sighed, "This is very interesting. I have heard stories of the Spanish Inquisition."

"Oh, yes. We are infamous for that as well. After the Christian reconquest of the Iberian Peninsula, it became dominated by Christians, but other religions continued to coexist. Even the Muslims were not totally driven out. Cities like modern-day Barcelona had a considerable Jewish population. Even the Muslims were tolerated but slowly their power decreased, and they ceased to hold any position of importance. The Catholics who ruled in the beginning were fairly tolerant of other religions, considering the times they lived in. The Jews especially continued to enjoy prominent posts in both politics and religion in Aragon."

"Unfortunately, in the Middle Ages, antisemitism was the norm in Europe. You may be surprised to know that even England and France expelled their Jewish populations.

Once Christians reconquered Spain, antisemitism prevalent in the rest of Europe increased. There were riots in cities like Barcelona. Jews were persecuted. Almost all Jews who remained had to change their religion and convert to Christianity in order to conceal their identity and escape persecution."

"Anyway, coming back to the Spanish Inquisition, at the time it was created, Castile and Aragon were the two mighty kingdoms of Spain. Attempts were made to unite both kingdoms. There is a romantic story associated with Isabella of Castile. She was also the half-sister of King Henry IV of Castile."

Henry said, "This becomes interesting. In Britain, a King called Henry IV was a true Bluebeard. He had six wives and a very interesting history. But do tell me more about the romance."

Jose smiled. His eyelids flickered. He began with a lazy drawl, "My generation had a weakness for romance. Everything was forgiven if people were in love. Looks like some of it has rubbed onto you as well."

Henry interrupted, "You were talking about Isabella of Castile."

Jose resumed his story, "Ah yes, being the heir of Castile with a stepbrother as ruler of England, she was very important. Therefore, her marriage too, was a diplomatic endeavour. There were marriage proposals from Portugal, France and Aragon. At that time, women in her position hardly had any say in their marriages. Her half-brother favoured Alphonso II from Portugal. Isabella, however, refused to consent to the marriage. A civil war almost broke out in Castile, shaking Henry's throne. In order to negotiate peace with the rebels, Henry arranged Isabella's unwilling marriage to Pedro Girón Acuña Pacheco, Master of the Order of Calatrava. Fortunately for Isabella, the groom passed away before the marriage. So, she was saved in answer to her prayers. The story goes that she wanted to marry her cousin Ferdinand of Aragon and secretly got engaged to him. Henry tried to get her married to a French prince, but Isabella was adamant. There was another hitch. Isabella and Ferdinand were second cousins and hence, their marriage would not be considered legal. However, they managed to obtain a papal decree. Since Isabella knew that Henry would never consent to their marriage, she decided to elope."

Henry murmured, "It would have been a very bold move during those times."

"Yes, but then Isabella in many ways, was way ahead of her times. Anyway, she went away from the court, giving the excuse that she wanted to visit her brother's tomb in Avila. Ferdinand, too, crossed Castile disguised as a servant. They were finally married in the city of Valladolid."

"So, a happy ending."

"Yes, kind of. Anyway, after Henry's death, Isabella came to the throne. She proved to be a capable ruler and even rode herself at the head of her army to suppress a rebellion. Anyway, I was talking about the Spanish Inquisition."

He paused to catch his breath and then continued; his eyes half closed, "Isabella and Ferdinand were both Catholic

Monarchs. Hence, they were interested in unifying their respective kingdoms and making it a military as well as a political power. This is perhaps one of the main reasons why the Spanish Inquisition came into being. Since the Catholic religion was one of the few things common to both kingdoms, Isabella and Ferdinand decided to use it to strengthen the laws of the land which could override the interests of the nobility. They felt the nobility and other vested interests could have no objection to it. It would also give them the power to deal with not only supposedly those who were considered religious heretics but also conspirators and political opponents or people who went against royal authority. Many members of high rank in the clergy and nobility were some of the first to be questioned by the Inquisition. The Inquisition also acted as some sort of judicial arm in both countries, trying anyone who violated the laws. Prior to the Inquisition, the Spanish were notorious for being bad Christians as they allowed several religions to coexist. Jews and Moors were also a part of the court. The Spanish Inquisition helped to remove the so-called taint. Antisemitism and racism were prevalent all over Europe and came to Spain too. In its very first case, six people were burnt alive. The Spanish Inquisition made Spanish Royalty even more powerful. However, one fact remained. The Inquisition could hold power only over Christians. Members of other religions were not within its preview but were harassed until they were either forced to leave or convert. Those who refused went through an agonizing and cruel death. They were burnt at the stake. Antisemitism continued to reign till mid-1530, after which it gradually reduced."

Henry said, "What about Protestants and those who strayed from the path of being devout Catholics?"

"Actually, the number of Protestants was fewer in number as compared to other countries in Europe. However, even among the Catholics, people were punished because of sins like sodomy and unnatural marriage. A marriage was termed unnatural if the union did not produce children. Criminal offences were also punished. Although it dealt with what was termed as religious offences, its main use was to increase the power of the crown. You won't believe, that though the Inquisition was medieval in concept, there were certain rules it followed. No person could be subjected to torture unless all other means had failed. Even if a person was tortured, there was a time limit set and the doctor remained on standby to meet any medical emergency. When Napoleon came to power, the Spanish Inquisition was abolished. However, it got a new temporary lease of life when the monarchy came back to power. As late as the mid-nineteenth century, a schoolteacher Cayetano Ripoll was executed for preaching what was then considered as deist principles. He may have been the last to be executed. Slowly, the Spanish Inquisition came to an end."

It was Henry's last night on the farm. Rosa had stirred up what he felt was a delicious feast. She had talked gaily, but Henry could discern a sadness in her eyes.

Alfred had said, "So you will be leaving us tomorrow?"

"Yes. I have written to the officials of my battalion. I'll start early in the morning."

Jose said, "We will miss you, boy. These last few days have been pleasant. I had a companion to talk to. It can be lonesome out here with the war. My brother lives nearby, but he can hardly visit us. Roads are dangerous. You never know when something will hit you. Half the bridges and roads do not exist anymore. So, it's damned difficult to move about."

Rosa said, "Come, let us talk of something pleasant. I'll get wine. We have some left in our cellar. Let's celebrate today. Tomorrow will be different."

It was. All of them gathered to bid him farewell. Henry thanked each of them for their hospitality. He exchanged hugs with Alfred and Jose.

Jose said with a catch in his voice, "Do take care of yourself. Hope we meet again."

Rosa clasped his hand warmly and said, "If you are anywhere near, do come to meet us."

Henry looked into Rosa's green eyes. There seemed to be a hint of tears in them.

He said lightly, "With the wonderful food you have given me, I will be looking for chances to come here again soon. Your cooking alone will draw me here."

Rosa smiled and said, "Take care. I will never forget these days."

Alfred asked the most practical question, "How will you reach your camp?"

Henry said, "Don't worry. I'll find my way."

Alfred said, "Walk up to the next village. I can accompany you till there. From there, you can take a bus ride to Madrid."

There was a lump in Henry's throat. He swallowed and said, "Thank you, but I will find my way. You are one of the best families I have come across in my lifetime. I am alive and can walk because of you. I will never forget these days of love and care. It had a dream-like quality about it."

He waved goodbye and then walked away without looking back. All the time, he felt a choking sensation as if his heart would burst. He knew the family would be waving till they saw the last of his receding figure. He walked on, determined not to look back.

It took two days to reach his camp. He was welcomed with unexpected warmth.

Miguel gave him a tight hug and said with tears in his eyes, "We gave you up for dead. No one knew where you were. We did look for a couple of days. There was no sign of you or even your body. I thought you must have fallen into the ravine."

Henry smiled, "Well, here I am in one piece."

Miguel said, giving him another hug, "Tell me your story. What happened to you?"

Henry told him. He mentioned Rosa but did not tell him about her beauty and bright eyes.

Henry could not sleep. He tossed and turned, but sleep did not come. Rosa's face floated in front of his eyes. Her green eyes seemed to beckon him. Her curly red hair tumbled down on her shoulders, giving her a reddish halo. Her soft smile lit up her face. He felt a fierce longing for her, a desire to see her again; just a glimpse of her would be enough. He kept thinking of Rosa until he fell asleep.

The next morning, Miguel handed him a letter. "The letter was lying with me. It came when you were sick. In my excitement of seeing you, I forgot to give it to you yesterday. It must be important. It's from India."

Henry took the letter and tore open the envelope. It was written in his nanaji's fine handwriting. He sat down under a tree to read it. At least there was no one here to disturb him.

'My dear Henry,

I am so happy to learn that you have gone to participate in the Spanish civil war. I strongly feel every able-bodied man should do so. I would have done so if I was young and strong instead of being a tottering old man whom God may call anytime soon.

I am happy, but your nani is not. She is upset and worries about you. She has written a strongly worded letter to your mother for allowing her son to go to the front. Why did she not stop you? Do write back about your welfare. It will assuage her fears. She spends a lot of time in the prayer room praying for your welfare. I can see tears flowing down her cheeks. She even consulted a pandit and a local astrologer to find ways to bring you back. I am afraid of her falling sick without reason harbouring what seems to me to be unreasonable fears.

I don't have any fears at all. I know that God will keep you safe. I am proud of you for offering your services to the Republicans. There is no better thing to do at this time. In India, everyone here is following the happenings in Spain with interest. I am doing so. I get all the information from the newspaper columns. We all feel that the British government has acted like a coward. Neville Chamberlain will go to any extent to avoid war with Hitler, who marches from strength to strength. Most European countries along with the United States are toeing the same line. The League of Nations is completely useless. It does not take sides and watches the events of the world as a mute spectator. This war can be over quickly if these countries support the Republican cause. It is the people of Spain who suffer like we Indians continue to do so under British rule.

You know my views on it. India still struggles for freedom in the true sense of the word. We are still miles away from not only political freedom but also social and economic freedom. You are not alone in fighting for the Spanish cause. Thousands in our country would do the same. When I told my friends that you had joined the International Brigade, they patted my back and congratulated me. One of them said, "Your grandson is doing a great job. He is fighting the fascists." I felt thrilled. You are doing fine work. At present, what can bring greater honour than treating the sick and the wounded?

You know what our famous leader Jawaharlal Nehru said about the Spanish civil war. I have read about it in the newspaper. I have kept the cutting of the speech. He made the speech way back in December at the annual National Congress meet. He said, and I quote his words as reported in the newspaper. "In Spain today, our battles are being fought and we watch this struggle not merely with the sympathy of friendly outsiders but with the painful anxieties of those who are themselves involved in it."

You will be interested to know that not only Nehru and other politicians but also the great bard of India, Rabindranath Tagore, has written on the subject. I quote him, "In Spain, the world civilization is being menaced and trampled underfoot. Against the democratic government of the Spanish people, Franco has raised the standard of revolt. International Fascism is pouring men and money in aid of the rebels… The devastating tide of International Fascism must be checked… At this hour of the supreme trial and suffering of the Spanish people, I appeal to the conscience of humanity. Help the peoples' front in Spain, help the Government of the people, cry in a million voices 'Halt!'… Come in your millions to the aid of democracy, to the succour of civilization and culture."

In India, our fight is progressing but slowly. The Congress led by the great Mahatma Gandhi continues to fight for Independence. The best thing about it is that the masses are involved. They are active participants and not mute spectators. Gandhi Ji attracts more and more followers daily. Many are prepared to make great sacrifices for the freedom of the country. Some of the Congress' leaders have gone to prison. There is progress. We have been given more say in the administration of the country. There are more Indians involved, but this is hardly enough. In the provincial elections, Congress has a majority. The clamour for complete Independence grows, and I hope to live to see the day when we live and breathe as a free nation with the Indian flag fluttering in the sky. There are undercurrents of trouble and it is not only from the British. In our neighbourhood, things seem okay, but I have noticed an undercurrent of suspicion between communities, which is tragic. I hope this does not ultimately lead to a bloodbath.

The other day, one of my friends voiced this suspicion. The hope that India, with all its religious and caste differences, will present a united front is still a far cry. It remains a deeply divisive society with many contradictions which seem difficult to overcome. Many feel that if war breaks out in Europe, which is likely, then India will be forced to be a part of it. It will mean loss of life and delay in getting independence.

Coming again to the Spanish Civil War, I must say a few Indians are helping the cause. Our political leaders and many of our fellow citizens believe it is a fight between forces of light like democracy and forces of darkness like fascism. The India League operating from Britain has played a major role in sending humanitarian aid to the Republicans. V.K Krishna Menon, a friend of Nehru, is its secretary. He wrote, "The freedom of the Indian people was synonymous with the freedom of the peoples of the world, and that imperialism and exploitation must end." The Spain-India Committee has donated an ambulance to help Spain.

You may have come across a few Indians. I always make it a point to read any write-up related to Spain in all newspapers and magazines. You know how much I love to read. There is a man named John Smith who is actually *Huddar*, an Indian from Gujarat who joined the International Brigade. Then, there is a journalist called Krishna. He is in Spain. He lives in England like you. He sends his articles to about 50 newspapers in India without charging any money. His actual name is Mulk Raj Anand. A staunch patriot, he also writes in favour of Indian Independence. I like his style of writing and I feel he will be a great writer one day. Three other Indian doctors are rendering selfless service to the Spanish cause: Dr Atal Mohanlal, Ayub Ahmed Khan Naqshbandi and Manuel Pinto.

Selfless service for people you don't know is one of humanity's most extraordinary acts. What all of you are doing in whatever capacity you can deserves the highest praise. However, nothing can equal what Norman Bethune is doing in Spain. He is a towering personality. There is so much about him in the papers. I make it a point to read it. He has given up what I consider a very lucrative job to help Spain. He is, of course, a true communist at heart. I have read that he was a member of the Communist Party in Canada. He intensely hated the commercial angle of medicine. He felt doctors who made money from their profession were a bane to society. You know, even when he arrived in Spain, despite his awesome reputation, he was not exactly welcomed with open arms. The authorities felt that a man of his abilities – a thoracic surgeon – was unnecessary. Another handicap he faced was his lack of knowledge of the Spanish language, which made communication difficult. It was only after he set up the mobile blood transfusion unit in Madrid that his fame and acceptance spread. However, I believe even today, though adored by the Spanish people; he still has run-ins with the authorities. Many of them dislike him for what they feel is his high-handedness. However, he continues doing what he feels is right with contempt for the military bureaucracy and administration interfering in his work. But, of course, you know these things since you are in Spain at the very heart of the war. As I bid you adieu, I can only say to take care of yourself and others. Your nani sends you her love. She has made a special request. Please have your meals on time, though I know it is impossible with the kind of work you are doing. Tell me all about your life in Spain. I am waiting to hear from you.

Your loving,

Nanaji

CHAPTER 8

Henry read the letter twice. He couldn't believe the words that were written. His grandfather, who had hitherto very little to say about him, had actually praised him sky-high. Unlike his parents, his grandfather supported him and had even given him a pat on his back. Tears pricked Henry's eyes which threatened to overflow. He tried to blink them away. If anyone saw him, they would think him unmanly.

He remembered when he first broached the subject of having joined the International Brigade to his parents; his father had changed colour. His lips quivered, his eyes glinted and a reddish pallor appeared on his face. Henry knew that his father was furious.

"What do you mean by saying you joined the International Brigade? It's the most foolhardy thing that I have heard about."

Henry stood his ground. His chin jutted out. He said, "I felt it was the right thing to do."

His father raised his voice, "What are you saying? You did not even ask us before joining up. You mean you are going to leave college?"

Henry answered in a steady voice, "At present, yes. I can always rejoin when the war is over."

His father raised his voice, "I would like to know who has influenced you?'

Henry said, "No one. I made the decision myself."

His voice heavy with sarcasm, his father said, "It is impossible to believe such a fairy tale. This is not even our war. It's Spain's business. Our government is neutral. Why the hell do you have to go and fight on foreign soil?"

Henry answered passionately, "It is foreign soil, but it is a fight for the very existence of democracy. If all freedom-loving people do not stand up for the Republicans now, the world will enter a dark age where dictators like Hitler and Mussolini call the shots. Hitler feels that Spain is his playground. If we don't stop Hitler now, it will be too late and the entire world will be plunged into darkness. There will be devastation and ruin, and men will become enslaved. Anyone of non-Aryan descent will be a second-rate citizen. I am going to fight for what I feel is right. I am fighting for a just world order. It does not matter which country you belong to. We will all be fighting for humanity."

His father's only answer was, "All poppycock."

Henry's mother was in tears. She pleaded with her son not to go, as it would break her heart. Her tears affected Henry and he found himself promising his mother to come back soon. "I will write to you regularly. There is very little risk. I am not going as a soldier but as a stretcher bearer."

As the day of his departure came near, his parents were more resigned to his decision. His father was unhappy but knew that Henry would not change his mind. In the end, when Henry was leaving, he relented enough to say, "I know you are making a ghastly mistake, but I wish you all the best. Take care."

His mother had said, "I will pray to God every day to keep you safe. I will go to the temple daily. Never forget to take your meals on time and wash your clothes." Her voice broke and she could not go any further as tears overflowed. After that, Henry walked out of his home towards what he felt was his destiny.

The letter had made him sentimental. It is never good to be sentimental. He had troubles enough. The image of Rosa kept coming to his mind; he just could not drive it away. Her flashing green eyes which lit up when she smiled, her red hair which shone like molten gold when the sunlight fell on it, her full-throated laughter, the graceful movement of her hands and her soft touch. He wished he could banish these thoughts from his mind. Somewhere he felt an aching sense of loneliness. Henry gave himself a mental shake. What was wrong with him? How could he feel lonely when he was always surrounded by people? Such feelings were never there in him before. He was upset a lot of times and angry at times but never actually bored. Why, he did not even have time to think. The moment he was free from work, he would fall asleep wherever he was without time to reflect even on the horrors he had witnessed. He was usually too drained of energy to do anything, even letting thoughts creep into his head.

Life was anything but monotonous and predictable. Anything could happen at any time. His work was the same, carrying the wounded and sick and attending to them in whatever way possible, but the people and places differed. Every day, he was assigned a different camp. So were the situations he had to face. Today, when he carried an injured man to the camp, he heard a Spanish doctor say angrily, "It's all Norman Bethune's fault."

The doctor had come out and met Henry carrying the unconscious patient who had just lost his arm. He said, still irritated, "Carry him right inside the camp to a bed although there are only a few of them."

Henry did so. Fortunately, his patient could get a spare bed; otherwise, he would lie on the floor with countless others. As he came out, he met the irate Spanish doctor murmuring, "That Bethune!"

At first, Henry thought he would not probe into what had angered the doctor. But he had heard Bethune's name spoken in heat and he wanted to know more. Curiosity goaded him to try to speak with the doctor, even at the risk of ticking him off.

He said, "Forgive me. I heard you speaking of Norman Bethune. What has he done?"

"What has he done? What has he not done, you might ask?'

"Do you know him?'

"Know him? What a stupid question to ask. Everyone here has the misfortune to know him. I often rue the day he set foot in Spain. He should have stayed in Canada where a man of his talents could be useful, but not here."

Henry waited and then asked, "You seem angry with him?"

The doctor, who had a thin pencil-lined moustache and sandy floppy hair, said, "I have good reason to be. He gets us into trouble. He rubs all the senior doctors the wrong way. He is extremely high-handed as if he is the man in charge, which he cannot be. He is new here. Spain is different from Canada. Every doctor and surgeon must follow the rules, or there will be trouble. The military bureaucracy that controls the war hates it. They dislike their decisions being overridden. Remember, boy, here in Spain, you have to follow certain protocols and show respect to authority by toeing their line. You just cannot pooh-pooh them away like how Norman Bethune is doing. These are time-tested rules. On top of it, he has a quick temper which he cannot control. When he loses it, the poor fellow at the receiving end finds it hard to digest."

Henry kept quiet. He did not know how to answer. The doctor may get even more angry.

The doctor continued, "He does not realize that it is we who have to face the backlash for his behaviour. The authorities give us a dressing down. The other day, I was called to the head office. The admin in charge said, 'Why do you allow the foreigner to run roughshod over our rules? He may be ignorant, but you know. He is here to help us out and not to create more trouble. You are Spanish, aren't you? You know how we do things here.'

I could only mutter, 'Yes, sir.' You cannot argue with your superiors.

The man said, 'Then keep him under a leash.'

I just said, 'He does not listen. You see, he has come with a reputation.'

'The more the reason for being compliant. Tell him if he wants to survive in Spain, he has to follow certain rules and learn to obey his superiors. He is a doctor, not the man in charge. You set him right.'

He does not realize that it is impossible to do so. Bethune has a king-sized ego. He is not the kind to listen. Sometimes, even basic courtesies escape him. On top of it, he has very little knowledge of Spanish. How can you explain anything to a man who does not understand the language and does not make any attempt to understand it either?"

Henry nodded sympathetically. He wanted the doctor to go on.

"You appear to be a bright lad. From your appearance, I can make out you are not Spanish either, but you understand what I say."

Henry said, "Yes, perfectly. I did learn Spanish."

"That's good. Coming back to Bethune. It's his total disdain for authority that is the trouble. The other day, he was going to operate. I told him that he had to get permission to do so. He gave me an angry glance and said, 'To hell with you. This man will be dead if I wait to take permission.' I felt hurt. This was no way to speak to a Spanish doctor. I don't know what he wants, but I feel he wants to be the boss. That is not possible. Besides, how can you reason with a man who drinks like a fish?"

Henry looked at him with startled eyes. The doctor continued gleefully, "You did not know that. Ah, yes, he is a heavy drinker. How can you reason with such a man? Besides, there is always the problem of women."

Henry put in hesitatingly. "I heard that he was married twice."

"Yes, to Frances. But it was not happy both times. They parted ways. Maybe she is the only woman that Bethune truly loved but there have always been women in his life. His name has been linked with several. I doubt he loved any of them. He may have loved Frances, but he spent her money quickly enough, following an extravagant lifestyle. During his first marriage with her, Frances inherited some money. The couple quickly ran through it. Bethune bought expensive art pieces, wore good clothes and went on a European honeymoon. He also studied. Soon, he ran out of her inheritance."

Henry knew the question was inappropriate, but he could not help asking as curiosity gnawed, "Is there anyone in his life now?"

"But, of course. He is never without a woman. At present, he is going around with a Swedish journalist, Kasja Rothman. She is exerting her influence in his affairs and Bethune lets her."

The doctor suddenly seemed to recollect himself. He was gossiping with a mere stretcher bearer. "Enough of tittle-tattle. Now, get going. I have no time for idle hands."

Henry bowed his head and ran out. He had learnt a lot of things about Norman Bethune. Did the man revered as God by the people of Spain have clay feet? Who was the real Norman Bethune? He did not know. Perhaps, he would never know.

CHAPTER 9

Henry could not forget Rosa. There was a strange ache in his heart whenever he thought of her, which was often. Her image kept floating in his mind. He thought of her peach and milk complexion, which always wore a tanned look because of long hours of exposure to the sun.

There was a longing in his heart to see her again; just a glimpse would suffice. The probability seemed unlikely. He would probably never see her again. The thought made him depressed.

Miguel had said one day, "What's wrong with you? You are not your usual self. Is there any bad news from home?"

Henry shook his head, mumbling, "No, nothing of that kind. I am fine."

Miguel retorted, "No, you are not. I can see that. Something has changed. I don't know what."

Henry kept quiet. It was all the same, except he knew that he had a deep longing for Rosa. However, Henry felt he could not reveal his innermost thoughts to anyone. Again, he thought, was his feeling for Rosa love? He did not know. Did Rosa spare even a moment's thought on him? Again, he did not know the answer to that either. He felt he would never know. From whatever he has seen of Rosa, he thought it would be difficult to fathom her true feelings for anyone. Despite her open-mindedness, there was a peculiar sense of allure that lingers on the outskirts of her heart, waiting to be acknowledged. Henry whispered once more, questioning, "Could this be love or just infatuation?"

He had gone to Madrid after a few days. There had been another bombing – the work of German planes. The undoubted air superiority of the Nationalists was only because of their heavy reliance on the German Luftwaffe.

Miguel said while running, "I don't know why they drop bombs on working-class quarters. The more affluent areas of Madrid are spared."

Henry answered, "The rich and super-rich, even the conservatives and most Catholics, are solidly behind Franco. Therefore, they avoid bombing these areas. Why should they dig their own grave?"

Miguel suddenly said, "The family you were staying with were Catholics, weren't they?"

Henry answered shortly, "Yes, devout ones. But they were backing the Republicans. They are small farmers with a bit of land."

They had almost reached Madrid. Henry, who was in Madrid after four weeks, was shocked by the changes yet again. Who would say it had any resemblance to the glorious Madrid of the past, which was culturally rich and famous for its Royal Palace, Alhambra, Casa Battlo, Alcazar of Seville and Santiago de Compostela Cathedral? These were places tourists who visited the city flocked to see from different parts of the world. There were no more tourists now. Almost all foreigners in Spain belonged to the International Brigades. Armed forces from Germany and Italy as well as some international volunteers, supported Franco. Parts of the city were in shambles. What was formerly a gay shop doing business had only a single wall standing. The rest of it had been ripped apart. Beside it stood another house. Perhaps, they had done up the walls. A piece of the new wallpaper fluttered on the remains of a half brick wall while all that remained of the woodwork were ashes. Henry glanced inside. Another half-broken brick wall stood with a few utensils, a pot and a lonely pan lying on the ground, sparkling new, which had miraculously survived the bombing. Perhaps, the house belonged to a newly wedded couple. They had done up the kitchen and house together, investing their savings and planning their future. It had all come to nought. God knew if the couple were living or dead. They had paid the penalty of war.

The city wore a run-down look. Half of the workers' quarters were gutted. A workman squatting near one of the houses said sobbing, "I had gone out to get food. When I returned, it was all over. My wife and parents are somewhere below this debris. I can't find even their bodies or their shattered limbs. If you have come to help, it is too late. I have escaped, but of what use is life to me?"

Henry picked up an eleven-year-old boy who was still alive and brought him to the nearest camp. The sun was about to set. He had made countless trips and was tired. He was trudging to his camp when he caught sight of her. Her back was to him as she was earnestly bargaining with a shopkeeper. There was no mistaking her. Her pile of red hair was pinned on top of her head. She was wearing a cream-coloured shirt. The hem of her green skirt almost trailed on the floor.

Before he could stop himself, he had called out, "Rosa."

She turned around. She looked as beautiful as ever. Her green eyes lit up in recognition and her lips curved in a broad smile on her flushed face.

Her lips opened in a cry, "Henry." She extended her hand to his and said, "How are you?"

Henry held her hands in a tight clasp. "I am fine, thanks to you. What are you doing here?"

"I had come to purchase groceries."

"Alone?"

"No, with friends. They dropped me here. We came in a van which goes once a week to Madrid."

"How are Alfred and Jose?"

"As well as they will be. Alfred is thinking of volunteering. Not as a soldier, just at the back end. Maybe logistics. It is yet only a thought. He has not done anything about it as yet."

"That's ok."

"He has also taken a new step. He has responded to the appeal made by Norman Bethune to donate blood. He went to a blood donation camp and did so. Alfred felt good. He told me that he felt he had done something concrete for the country."

"It is very creditable."

"Are you taking care of yourself? Are you eating well?"

"Yes, I am."

"You are here for work? Forgive me, what a stupid question to ask."

"No, it is not. But you are right. The war is on."

A voice called, "Rosa, you are getting late."

"I must hurry or I will miss the van. We live in uncertain times."

Henry wanted to say more, but the chance was lost. Rosa hurried back.

Miguel, standing nearby, looked at the ground and said, "Is this the girl who looked after you?"

Henry said, his face flushed, "Yes."

"It is obvious that you care for her. Have you talked to her?"

"No," Henry muttered, his eyes downcast, avoiding eye-to-eye contact with Miguel.

"Then, you had better ask it soon. She is a beauty. With her good looks, she will soon be snapped by someone else and you will be left twiddling your thumb."

Henry did not answer. What could he do? Times were far from normal. He was always on the move from one camp to another. It was by sheer chance that he had met her today. When would he get another chance? How could one even attempt to court a girl in these uncertain times when not even one minute was predictable? A strange melancholy settled in him. He may never see Rosa again or tell her how he feels. How soft were her hands when he had clasped them! There was a warmth in them. Was she as thrilled to see him as he was to see her? Her face was flushed and there was a warmth in her eyes. But was it the pleasure of meeting a friend or something more? He did not know. It was now dark, the moon half hidden in the clouds, played hide and seek, casting eerie shadows. It was just a fragment of a moon that showed its face at times. Half the street lights had already shattered and the rest were dimmed for the fear of bombing. Residents were also encouraged to switch off their lights most of the time. Somewhere, he could hear the sound of a shell bursting and the glass on a window plane crackling. People on the sidewalk looked up, startled, trying to discern the distance and then went about their activities. Such sounds had become the new normal in Madrid. Henry went past a café. It was full. The lights were blazing and he could hear gay laughter as people sipped their drinks. Life went on. Many accepted death and destruction as something usual and tried to snatch moments of pleasure and happiness in the midst of ruin.

CHAPTER 10

Henry woke up with a start. He had fallen asleep on a straw mattress on the stone floor of a half-broken house. Another newcomer joined them. He was a red-faced man with a pencil-thin moustache and very little hair. Henry guessed his age was over 40. He introduced himself, "Guys, I am Edgar. I am new here in this camp, I mean. I joined the International Brigades in the medical field as a technician. I had the honour of serving Norman Bethune. I saw his work in a sub-branch of the Madrid centre. It is pretty well organized."

Henry asked, "Do you know how it began?"

"I have heard from my colleagues how he started it all, the mobile blood transfusion, I mean. The centre was, of course, Madrid. He was allotted a palatial apartment in Principe de Vergara, one of the wealthy localities of Madrid, for his work. This was one of the good things that the Spanish government did. It was a good move as the Nationalists avoided dropping their deadly cargo in these localities. So, it was a reasonably secure area to work in. Leaving aside three rooms which served as living quarters of the Canadian delegation, the others were turned into rooms used for medical purposes like refrigeration rooms for storing blood and another for blood transfusion. The equipment for transfusion and refrigeration units had been installed.

He jokingly dubbed it as 'milk delivery system.' Bethune knew that he would need volunteers who would donate blood; otherwise, the system would not work. The press and radio were brought into play, and for three consecutive days, an appeal went out. Blood was urgently required to save the lives of soldiers fighting for the cause. On the third day, I believe Bethune had surveyed the equipment ready to be used. The new bottles stood in the refrigeration room and the beds for donors and equipment stood in the transfusion room, ready to be used. I have heard from the Spanish doctor who was at that time by his side that suddenly Bethune felt the jitters like any normal human being would before starting a new venture. What if nobody turned up to donate blood? Without donors, his project would be useless. However, he need not have worried. There were over two thousand people who had come to donate blood. They included both men and women, old and young. More people continued walking in, willing to donate their blood."

Miguel, who was listening with rapt attention, said, "It must have been a scene to be believed. The doctor's expression would be worth watching."

"According to the Spanish doctor I talked to, his face betrayed no expression. However, the entire unit set to work at once, registering names, screening the donors, and making the requisite malaria and syphilis tests. All the standing bottles were filled. Even the kitchen refrigerator was emptied and a makeshift storage space was created. Finally, there were no more bottles left to fill with blood. The milling crowd outside was still eager to donate and disappointed and irate when they heard that all the blood they needed had been taken. There was no need for their blood.

But the angry crowd continued to push, exclaiming in Spanish, 'Take our blood. Our men fighting in the front need it.'

The harassed Spanish doctor had turned to Bethune to find a way out. Bethune is believed to have suggested registering all their names and taking their blood tests. He assured the crowd that their blood would be taken after a few days. This calmed the crowd."

Henry interrupted, "When did the soldiers start getting blood?"

"Immediately. It was a huge success. A lot of lives were saved. Work was extended. Then, of course, the blood transfusion units were established all over the country near the battlefront. Most of them were located in hospitals – some in makeshift camps. I worked as a lab technician in one of them. Norman Bethune was not content to stay cooped up in Madrid. He visited the camps himself and plunged into work. I have seen his energy. It is seen to be believed. I have even talked to him one-to-one. He could be very friendly in the right mood, especially if you shared a drink. He was a great poet. I have read his poems. They are of a high calibre. Are any of you interested in poetry?"

Henry spoke up, "I am."

"So am I. I have got a few cuttings of his poems. You can read it if you want."

"I would love to."

He handed Henry the cutting of a poem published in a newspaper. It was written before Norman Bethune left for Spain.

'And this same pallid moon tonight,

Which rides so quietly, clear and high,

The mirror of our pale and troubled gaze,

Raised to a cool Canadian sky.

Above the shattered mountain tops,

Last night, rose low and wild and red,

Reflecting back from her illumined shield,

The blood bespattered faces of the dead.

To that pale disc, we raise our clenched fists,

And to those nameless dead our vows renew,

"Comrades, who fought for freedom and the future world,

Who died for us, we will remember you."'

Henry said, "It's very good. That a man can be so good in art as well as medical science is unbelievable."

"Ah, I see you are amazed. Here is another one. This was written when he was suffering from tuberculosis."

'Sweet death, thou kindest angel of them all,

In thy soft arms, at last, O let me fall;

Bright stars are out, long gone the burning sun.

My little act is over, and the tiresome play is done.'

Henry found one more. This time, it was about a woman. He read it with avid interest.

'Strike, if you strike must

But warm us first; it was better so to die

Beneath your fierce flames than perish in the shade

Cold and alone

Perhaps, a miracle as happened once, should come again

That golden glare was made to stand

And never sink and never leave the land

Desolate and dark

But stay, suspended overhead,

High, serene and clear

Perpetuate'

There was another on Remembrance

'Remembrance

I can't pretend

I think of you every hour; why

Such dull days I'm not aware of you at all,

Any more than the beating of my heart thru,

A young tree in the wind.

A white flower in the grass,

A quick bird in flight,

Like a cup turned upside down

But I can't pretend

This happens every day,

A breath of sun-named air,

And the whole world is emptied of delight

And I am hollowed and sick for my love,

But I can't pretend

This happens every day

My Pony.'

Edgar handed him another, saying, "This is recent. It concerns Spain. So, you would be more interested. This is about a bombing incident. You can see the pathos in his writing."

'Bombing of a hospital in the area of Madrid,

I came from CUATRO CAMINOS

From Cuatro Caminos, I come,

My eyes are overflowing,

And clouded with blood.

The blood of a little fair one,

Whom I saw destroyed on the ground;

The blood of a young woman,

The blood of an old man, a very old man,
The blood of many people, of many
Trusting, helpless,
Fallen under the bombs
Of the pirates of the air.
I come from Cuatro Caminos,
From Cuatro Caminos I come,
My ears are deaf
With blasphemies and wailings,
Ay little one, little one;
What hast thou done to these dogs
That they have dashed thee in pieces
On the stones of the grounds?
Ay, ay, ay, Mother, my mother;
Why have they killed the old grandfather?
Because they are wolf's cubs,
Cubs of a man-eating wolf.
Because the blood that runs in their veins
Is the blood of brothel and mud
Because in their regiment
They are born fatherless

A "Curse of God" rends the air

Towards the infamy of heaven.'

He was deep into the poems when there was a cry outside. "On your feet at once. Run to the front. We must go to Almeria. It has been battered and bombed. Many soldiers are injured."

Miguel asked, "How are we to get there?"

"A station wagon will take you. Get the first aid kit ready."

Almeria, by the side of the Mediterranean Sea, had an enchanting natural beauty, exquisite beaches, rugged cliffs and even a wild west desert. The sea was blue, with the glittering sun throwing golden shafts into its water. Had it not been for the war, it would have been a place of tourist attraction. However, there was an eerie quiet in the city punctuated by cries of agony. Many have been caught in the sudden shower of bombs. They failed to escape through the underground network of subterranean tunnels which the Republicans had built to provide a semblance of security to its citizens. Many soldiers were lying dead from shells that had hit them. Henry bent to see if any of them were injured. A soldier was lying on his chest. Henry could only see the back of the head. He was startled. It seemed familiar. He bent forward, his heart racing. He turned the body over. He had found Robert.

CHAPTER 11

Henry stared at Robert shell shocked. At first, he could not believe his eyes. But yes, there was no room for mistake. His face was unmistakable. His mass of blond hair was spread across his forehead, his lips slightly twisted in agony, and his grey eyes wore a dazed look. His shirt was bloody and Henry knew that a bullet had got him. He stood looking at him immobile.

A voice and a nudge on his chest said, "Move on, you fool. It is obvious that this guy does not need your help. He is dead."

He is dead…the words sunk into the recesses of his mind. Robert, his friend and companion of a not-so-distant past. He would never hear his roaring laughter, his passionate outbursts, his punting during a football match or his wild euphoric scream of "howzat" in cricket when he got a wicket – the way he threw back his head when he laughed, the rapid gestures of his hand when he was excited.

Tears welled in him, but he thought he had to think of the present. He could not give way to grief, at least not immediately. It would come later. He had to take care of the body, Robert's body.

Henry spoke, at last, the words bursting through him in a torrent, "I know him. This is Robert. He was my friend, my dear childhood friend."

Miguel, who was once again his partner, said, "What do you want to do? He is dead."

"I want to send his body home," Henry said with a catch in his voice.

Miguel nodded. They picked up Robert on a stretcher and came to the base hospital. Miguel said, "We have to approach someone of authority. They can tell us what to do and how to send his body home. Did he live in England?"

Henry nodded. His throat felt choked and he knew he could not burst out in tears until he made arrangements for the body. Poor, poor Robert. Henry thought it would be his greatest achievement if he could make arrangements to get Robert home. He went inside the hospital and asked for the man in charge. A bleary-eyed Spanish doctor came out.

Henry approached him, "*Hola. necesito ayuda.* This is my friend Robert. He is dead. I want to send him to England, his home."

The doctor took one look at Robert and said, "As a doc, I feel his body would decompose rapidly. However, since you sound sincere, I shall ask one of my seniors in the administration."

Miguel spoke, "Please do so. My friend here is distraught."

The doctor extended his hand with his palm facing up and said, "Don't move from here."

The Spanish doctor went inside and talked to someone. Another man came wearing a worn Republican uniform adorned with military badges. He said, "I am a colonel.

Give him a soldier's burial right here in the hospital yard. There is no other way. We simply can't send his body home. There is no such provision."

Henry pleaded, "Can't it be treated as a special case?"

The colonel shook his head, "No. Not now in Spain, where thousands of soldiers die every day. They are usually buried in mass graves right on the spot where they fall. These days, nothing much is possible. Your friend is fortunate that you have found him. He will have someone with him when he is lowered to the earth."

Henry again choked back his tears and turned to Miguel, "Will you help me?"

Miguel nodded. Together, they took Robert to the hospital yard. Fortune favoured them in another way. They found a large wooden box which could serve as a temporary casket. Then, they carried him to a corner of the yard where there was a grassy patch with a few wild violets. Using a garden shovel, they began digging. They felt exhausted but continued their task with sincerity. The box was lowered and Henry said the words which he could recall from memory, "We therefore commit this body to the ground, earth to earth, ashes to ashes, dust to dust; in sure and certain hope of the resurrection to eternal life."

At last, the task was over, and Robert had finally come to rest, but it was on Spanish soil. Henry picked up a few violets and placed them on the grave. He thought he would remember the place. He committed to his memory the name of the hospital. It was "Saint Louis." If ever there was such a possibility in future, he would take Robert back to his home and bury him again on English soil. He promised himself. He owed that much to his friend.

Now that the work was done, Henry felt tears that had well up deep inside him pour out in abundance. His shoulders heaved and his body shook. Sobbing, he fell on Miguel's shoulders, saying, "I will never hear his voice or see Robert again."

For a few minutes, Miguel let him cry. There was nothing he could say. He said quietly, "Come on, Henry. You have to pull yourself together. We have to go and attend to the living. There are hundreds who are waiting for our help. Maybe we can save theirs even though we could not save your friend's life."

Henry wiped his eyes and then stood up. Miguel was right. Grief was a luxury he could ill afford. For a moment, he had forgotten his duty. He had to help other soldiers.

When they had finished, Miguel asked, "Did you inform his home?"

Henry shook his head. "I will write tonight. I will have to arrange for pen and paper. We are living like vagabonds without anything."

At night, he obtained a pen and paper from the hospital. He wrote to the only person he knew who would be able to inform Robert's parents, Edwina. He knew what a painful task awaited her – informing Robert's parents that their son was dead. He had died a soldier's death and was now lying in a grave not in a cemetery but in a hospital yard without an epitaph. The glory of his death was not obvious. He had gone down fighting not for his country but for an idea – the idea of freedom and democracy. He sat down and wrote,

'Dear Edwina,

There is some really bad news. Our friend Robert....'

He finished the letter and then, closed his eyes. Sleep evaded him. He kept thinking of Robert and the time they spent together. If only he could share his grief with Rosa. He was sure she would give him a patient hearing, pat him on his shoulder or grasp his hand while her green eyes would mirror his sadness. Then, he thought, even in grief and shock, Rosa intruded into his thoughts. If this was not love, what was?

He did not know when he had fallen asleep. Perhaps, he slept out of sheer exhaustion. He was woken up with a shake. Someone was shaking him by his shoulder. His eyes flickered open. "Henry, Henry, we have to rush. There has been another tragedy. Malaga has been besieged. We have just received the orders to go there."

Henry was quick on his feet. He slipped into his blue overalls, took their stretcher and first aid kid and ran to the waiting truck, which would take them to the spot.

Miguel said, "Malaga was a Republican bastion. Its fall means one more victory for Franco."

While running, they met other stretcher-bearers.

Someone screamed, "These bloody fascists. They do not know any humanity. They have bombed refugees on the highway. I hope they rot in hell for what they have done."

Henry said, shocked to the core, "They must have been fleeing out of Malaga. Butchering refugees – your own countrymen – is the worst crime in humanity."

They had reached the Malaga-Almeria Road and stood there rooted to the ground. A swarm of people were heading to Almeria on the lone highway from Malaga. It was they who had been hit. The highway of tragedy, as Henry named it. If one lived in normal times, the highway would have been one of great scenic beauty. The road wound around the jagged coast. On one side were the cliffs, a tower of craggy grey rocks which stood in solid splendour, unperturbed by the events they witnessed. They had been standing in the same way for centuries, unmoved by whatever happened. On the left, these cliffs overlooked the Mediterranean Sea. The coast here was rocky and the gushing waves ran straight to the rocks only to retreat with a splash. The sun overhead was blazing in full glory, warming up the earth and all creatures on the highway.

It was the stream of people that caught Henry's attention. They were fleeing from Malaga with whatever belongings they could salvage. There were old men, women and children trudging wearily in the hot sun. A few donkeys and mules, their backs loaded with possessions consisting of meagre clothes, pots and pans, were making their way to Almeria in the hope of finding shelter. They were all refugees, rendered homeless walking in this blistering sun, often hungry and thirsty with festering wounds. A few amongst them, without footwear, were trudging wearily instead of walking, their feet bearing the painful marks of countless blisters. There were a few cars and trucks on the road as well. This sea of helpless humanity travelling almost shoulder to shoulder with each other on this lone escape route was fired upon by planes overhead and warships of the fascists, which had butchered them. Their bodies were lying heaped on the roadside. Those who were still alive walked on, circumventing these bodies. The only sounds he could hear were the wailing and screams of the wounded.

It was in the midst of ruin and the most inhuman act that he heard words which sounded the most interesting he had ever heard. "I have heard that Norman Bethune is already right here somewhere. This man is always there at the heart of horror, helping others."

It was another medico who had spoken. Henry looked at him keenly. Would he finally get a chance to meet the great Bethune himself?

CHAPTER 12

There was so much blood. Splashes of it adorned the road in grotesque patterns. It was difficult to distinguish between the dead and the living. Henry and Miguel examined each body and carried them away. A makeshift base camp had been set up on one side of the road where doctors armed with a few medicines and basic medical equipment were tending to the sick and wounded. There were too many of them. Henry did not have time to think for the next couple of hours as he ran, doing his best to stem wounds and carry them to help.

On the road sat a grizzled old man dressed in tattered clothes that had seen better days. He sat on his haunches with his head resting on his knees. He looked up suddenly. Crevices crisscrossed his wizened face, which peeped under a clumsily donned faded grey hat. His whole body seemed shrivelled, and his veins stood out from his arms. He had heavy eye bags and peered at Henry who was standing near him.

His voice was strangely authoritative when he spoke, "Boy, don't tire yourself out. You need a breather. You are human like the rest of us."

Henry looked into his face, startled. He thought this was perhaps the first man he met who showed concern for him. Usually, all the wounded and sick talked only of themselves. The old man spoke again, "You don't have a drink with you, do you? I am dying of thirst."

Henry shook his head. The old man continued, "They should have got me. But I survived once again. It was not a matter of chance that the bombs dropped where they did. It was deliberate. The dammed fascists knew what they were doing, murdering innocent people. This is not war – it is murder, a barbaric crime which has no parallel in history. I saw the planes myself. They swooped down and dropped bombs. You could make out that they were deliberately targeting us. There was no room for mistake. Everyone on this road is a refugee, poor or rich. They have lost their homes, which have probably burnt to cinders. They have nothing but a few essential items – many of them carrying nothing with them but a few photographs of sentimental value, not even enough food. A woman I had become friendly with showed me the photograph of her son fighting in the front. It was the only thing she carried along with two pieces of bread. She is dead now. Strangely enough, I don't feel sorry for her. She went away quickly, perhaps spared from greater tragedies. If you live to be old, you see life at its worst. You will lose all your loved ones and survive when you wish you were dead."

Henry could not help saying, "You seemed to have suffered much."

The old man answered in a steady voice, "Aye, I have. Life means suffering. People fear death. I don't any more. One of the reasons is that I don't want to go on living. It is, at times, I feel a worthless exercise. I have lost all who were dear to me. My wife died of grief and depression. My two sons gave up their lives. What is there to live for? The only thing I enjoy are drinks, and even that is not easy to procure any more. A bottle of whisky sounds like heaven to me."

Henry answered with a catch in his voice, "Don't say such things. Life is always worth living. There is always someone who needs you, even if it is a person you don't know."

The old man shook his head, "Ah, you are young. You still have ideals. You have not lived the life that I have. Experience has made me bitter."

"It is the war."

"War is the most foolish thing man does. It brings suffering to all sides. There is actually no winner. Even those who are victorious are losers. I have been to the Great War. I was a soldier. I have heard that Adolf Hitler was a mere corporal in it. It was at that time that the aircraft was first used in warfare. Bombs fell even then and the civilians suffered, especially those who lived in big cities. The villages fared better but they, too, suffered. Dying of slow starvation can be worse than getting a bullet in your chest. It's not a quick death but a slow, lingering one. I fought for the Allies although my country remained neutral. I served as a soldier in the British regiment. You see, my in-laws were British, and I was living with them at that time. We were called Tommies, while we called the German soldiers Huns. Trench warfare hit us hard. We were trained in using arms, although not professional soldiers. Lying in the trench hour after hour can take a toll on you. The enemy was clever too. They would hit you when you least expect them to. I was there at Marne and the third battle of Ypres. It was a total rout. These Huns could be clever. I saw my comrades fall one by one. They who shared life with me, ate and drank with me. I loved my drink and despite scarcity, there was plenty available to us soldiers. That was one good thing about the war. When I saw my comrades fall one by one, it broke my heart. I was left alone then, and I am left alone now. Of course, we won but at what cost? Thousands of soldiers were killed – many who died were not soldiers but civilians, including women and children who had nothing to do with the war. I even pitied the Huns. A prisoner of war I talked to, a young lad still in his teens, said he did not know why he was fighting at all. I still remember his words, 'I was in school. My ambition in life was not to fight but to be an artist. I was never a fan of Kaiser Wilhelm II. I did not take much interest in politics and what Germany was doing. Then came the order that all able-bodied young men have to join. You were considered a traitor if you did not. So, I was sort of forced to join for the sake of the country. I can't say I felt any patriotic stirrings in me. I just did what I was ordered to by our leader. It was a question of survival. Now, here I am, a prisoner of war likely to be shot for no fault of mine.'"

"We did come out victorious, but the cost was too high in terms of human life and suffering. Economically, it is devastating. The rich and middle class become poorer and the poor are unable to survive. It's the women who suffer the most. They lose their husbands and sons. The occupying army rapes them. It is never good to go to war."

"Franco has made us go to war again."

"Franco is the devil incarnate – Satan at his worst. But you know he was not always like that. Who knows why he became the man he did? He never got along with his father, who married again. He trained at the Military Academy and went into the Army; his father was in the Navy, too, so I guess it was a sort of family tradition. At that time, perhaps he was a good boy. When he went to the Canary Islands, the devil entered into him. He became ambitious and lusted for power. Look what he has done to his own countrymen. Thousands have been tortured and even murdered in cold blood because they did not believe in his conservative ideals and supported the Republicans."

The old man shuddered.

Henry asked gently, "Now in Malaga?"

The old man nodded. "In Malaga, my house was destroyed in the bombing. I sometimes wish I was there trapped in the house and had died a quick death. I escaped because I had gone to another part of the town to visit friends. They had invited me for drinks and I am not a person to refuse such an offer. When I came back, it was all over. There was little that I could salvage from the wreck. There was no place called home anymore. There was panic all around. It seemed the whole city had gone crazy. Fear and grief were the predominant emotions. Screams and the sound of weeping filled the smoke-filled area coupled with coughing and spluttering. When I came back, the smoke hung like a low cloud on the ground. I was dry-eyed. I did not even shed tears. I had suffered too much in my life. The unpredictable had become predictable. Besides, I cannot call it unpredictable really. Malaga was a Republican stronghold. Almost the entire city supported the Republicans. Franco had his eyes on it for long. He was aided by the Italians and the German Condor Legion. There was no real resistance. Our anti-aircraft guns hardly made any noise. None of us wanted to stay back. We knew the retribution would be terrible. The atrocities would be unbearable and therefore, we felt; that anything would be better than staying back. I grabbed a bottle of drink and headed out. It's finished now. There was only one way out of the besieged city – the highway. Therefore, almost *en masse*, we headed for Almeria."

The old man wiped the sweat from his forehead with the back of his hand. "At that time, we did not know that almost everyone was thinking along the same lines. It was a scene to be believed. The entire highway was crawling with people making their way to Almeria. There were a few cars, but most of the people walked. I saw a man leading a donkey by the string. The donkey's back was laden with mattresses, blankets, a pile of clothes, pots and pans beside a water container. He carried a child on his back, tied tightly with a piece of ragged cloth. A woman followed, dragging her feet with a baby in her arms. Tears ran down her cheeks. They walked under the hot sun scorching the road with its piercing rays, hoping to reach Almeria, covering more than two hundred miles on foot – an impossible task for a family. Yet, they trudged on. They did not know what they would do once they reached Almeria. They had no place to stay, nor would they be welcome in any. They would be refugees there too. All they knew was that they were going to a place of relative safety. I do not know if that family survived the bomb attack. Countless such families must have perished. Their children will never see the light of the sun again or grow up in a more peaceful world. Again, I feel that growing up in a peaceful world is an impossible dream. There will soon be another World War, mark my words. All the signs are there. Once again, the root cause will be German ambition and aggression, just like in the First World War."

Henry said, "That's what I feel. This is one of the reasons why I joined the war. I felt Hitler needed to be stopped, or we will face a worse future than what we think now under Nazi world domination. I have gone through Mein Kampf, the book Hitler has written. His future plans are there for all to see."

"Yes, yes, but who is stopping him? The Republicans? No chance. France and Britain are neutral. They do not have the guts to take on Hitler head-on. We all know the reason why Franco is winning. If all other democratic countries, and I don't mean the International Brigades, had supported us, then perhaps, the Nationalists would have been defeated, and we would have won. Spain could have been saved from a catastrophe, and even Hitler would have thought twice before going for any misadventure."

Henry said, "Yes, you were talking about this highway."

"Ah, crammed with people it was. There were so many. You could see the men, their eyes listless, their scarred feet taking one step at a time, clutching a few family possessions. They were like the living dead clinging to hope with a thread. To keep their spirits up they sang,

'El Ejército del Ebro,
rumba la rumba la rumba la.
El Ejército del Ebro,
rumba la rumba la rumba la

Una noche el río pasó,
¡Ay Carmela! ¡Ay Carmela!
Una noche el río pasó,
¡Ay Carmela! ¡Ay Carmela!
Y a las tropas invasoras,
rumba la rumba la rumba la.
Y a las tropas invasoras,
rumba la rumba la rumba la

Buena paliza les dio,
¡Ay Carmela! ¡Ay Carmela!
Buena paliza les dio,
¡Ay Carmela! ¡Ay Carmela!'

The women trudged wearily, limping, sometimes carrying children, many of them walking with desperation simply to flee Malaga and walk towards what they felt was security. Many of them couldn't go further. There were women big with child, their bellies protruding, waddling slowly. The roadside became a hive of human activity. It saw both death and birth. Many women gave birth right on the road as they had no other alternative and their time had come. I do not know how many children were born on that highway. Plenty, I feel. They did not know what awaited them. The children were a bewildered lot, not knowing why they were made to walk for hours together under the hot sun without much food, leaving their home and everything familiar behind. People moved like ghosts of their former selves, hardly making a sound. They were too weary to talk or even cry except for an occasional scream of pain. There were thousands of us walking. Many who could not go on lay down by the roadside to die. I doubt if the pilots of the bombers could see even an inch of the road. I do not know how many of them are still living after the horrifying attack on them. Perhaps, it is better to be dead than to live like the dead. I wish I had died, but I survived."

Henry said, "Truly, it is hopeless."

The man shook his head, "There is one hope. That is Norman Bethune. He is here."

Then without warning, a cry went out among all medicos. "Bethune is here and he needs all our help. Get ready, boys, and help him. He will be our saviour yet. I have heard that he has a large truck. He has already ferried countless children to the Almeria hospital where medical treatment awaits them."

Henry looked up. Leaving the old man squatting on the highway and with a stretcher in his hand, Henry ran towards the senior medic officer calling. At last, he was going to be face-to-face with Norman Bethune.

CHAPTER 13

He came in a huge ambulance. Henry saw a middle-aged man of medium height with a sprinkle of grey hair on a bald head alighting from the ambulance. He had an erect bearing with a military moustache. In his hand was a black bag and a medical kit. He stood there barking orders.

He told a man, "Remove all the bottles of blood and pack as many people as you can. Tell the hospital authorities or whoever you find that these people have to be evacuated. Tell them to send more trucks, vehicles, any dammed car or even carts on this road. Take my name. If that doesn't work, then tell them to move their asses from their chairs and get any help they can. More docs will be required. If none are available, then medicos will do. For God's sake - drill into their ears that they have to send help if they care an iota for their countrymen."

Henry noticed that two companions of Bethune were always at his side. He was to learn later that they were Hazen Sise, who worked as an ambulance driver and Thomas Worsley

Bethune then turned to Sise, "You drive as usual. After you reach the hospital and talk to the authorities, go straight to the governor's office. Ask them for more transport. Drive like hell without stopping once until you reach your destination. If some militiamen try to force you to stop, tell them to get lost."

The man addressed as Sise, just got into the ambulance without a word and started the engine.

The entire mass of humanity crowded around the ambulance, wanting to be taken to safety. Bethune again barked orders, his voice loud enough to be heard, "Just the children."

The scene was too tragic to be believed. Desperate mothers shoved their crying children into the ambulance. A sobbing mother said to her three-year-old daughter, who clung to her, "Go with them. You will be safe. Do not worry. I will find you." She knew the chances of finding her daughter again were remote.

A woman approached. She held a two-year toddler with one arm and with another raised her dress to reveal her protruding belly. She cried, "What about this unborn child? Does he or she count as a child? Will this child be able to survive without me?" She was hoisted inside.

Another woman with a tiny naked baby sucking at her breast said, "What about me? This baby was born right on the highway. He cannot live without my milk." She was taken into the ambulance. Bethune himself shut the door of the ambulance. The ambulance was fitted choc a block with children. The fortunate ones had benches to sit on. Others sat on the floor. The rest of them just stood wherever there was space, hoping to reach safety as the ambulance started its journey wading its way through crowds of people.

Henry was fortunate to see Norman Bethune at work. He stood at one end of the highway without watching the ambulance and, in the sweltering heat, started immediately tending to the sick and the wounded. No task was beneath him. He cursed the fascists, "The damned barbarians."

To Henry's surprise, he turned to him and said, "Do you know how to tie a bandage and dress a wound, boy?"

Henry nodded, stunned that he was addressed by the great Bethune.

"Then, do so. We have so few people who know how to."

Suddenly, as Henry bent over the next patient, Bethune's voice called out. "What's your name, boy?"

"Henry."

"Where are you from?"

"From England."

"Nice country but awful weather and politicians. I've lived there for some time. I am Norman Bethune." As if he needed an introduction.

Henry managed a weak smile. "Everyone here has heard about you."

There were thousands of patients. All of them needed attention. Many suffered from loss of blood. Bethune himself bent over a critical patient and transfused blood right on the roadside in primitive conditions but with sterilizing equipment.

He heard Bethune murmur, "This man needs it desperately." Almost like magic, a man lying on the road, pale and listless, revived like a wilted flower which received a fresh shower. As new blood pulsated in his veins, colour returned to the man's face and he was able to sit. Bethune patted his back and moved on. Henry could discern genuine concern on his face. It was, however, while treating children that Bethune was the most compassionate. Nothing seemed beyond his attention. Each child he attended to was with unbelievable tenderness.

Henry heard him saying, "It is they who are our future. They deserve our highest care and they have a right to grow up. They must be kept safe."

While treating children, he talked to them softly and handled them with a tenderness equal to any woman. He would even crack jokes to divert their attention from their agony.

He would say, "This war has been most brutal to children. They are suffering for no fault of their own. Many are orphans without anyone to take care of them. I have a plan for them. We could set up children's villages where these children would be taken care of and grow up in relative safety."

The ambulance came back again and was once again packed with children and a few women to take them relative safety. Once again, similar scenes were witnessed. People crowded around it, waiting to be taken to safety.

A sobbing mother told Henry, "I don't know if I will see my son again. He was clinging to my skirt all the way we were walking. I wish I could have gone with him too. He had only a ragged shirt on. A three-year-old child separated from his mother. You saw how he cried when he boarded the ambulance, clinging to me. I had to use force to wrench him off. I don't know if I will find him again. But he had to get a chance to live. We will surely die on this road. My feet are still bleeding."

Henry said, "I can help you there. I still have a few bandages left. It will stop the blood."

The woman sat quietly as Henry dressed her feet. The tears still fell. Henry knew that there could be no words of consolation.

Henry saw Norman Bethune helping an old woman with her head on her knees. Her legs were bleeding profusely. Norman Bethune took out a tube and bandages from his bag.

He gently bandaged her legs and said in English, "You will be able to walk again. Almeria is still a long way off."

The woman could not understand what Bethune was saying and simply nodded, a sign of gaunt resignation on her face. She, however, extended her hands, which Bethune clasped in a gesture of wordless thanks. Bethune lighted a cigar and puffed away. He stamped out the stub and bent over the next patient. Henry watched him, amazed at his dedication. Henry himself was tired. He felt like lying down and going to sleep, but Bethune worked tirelessly. His face had become pale and his sleep-deprived eyes popped out from their sockets, but he continued until almost the last bandage had been tied.

Soon, a more welcome sight met their eyes. It was Sise driving a van.

Bethune said, "I am never more glad to see you. Have you brought supplies?"

Sise nodded, "Oh, yes. Lots of them – Medicines, bandages, first aid, the works. You'll be happy for another reason too. I've brought your cigars as well."

Bethune nodded, "God knows I'll need them." He turned to a few subordinates who were standing near him, waiting for orders, "Don't stand there idling. Pack as many people as you can in this van. Now, you can take entire families. I hate it when families are broken – another tragedy of the war. They should be kept together for the sake of their children. Pack them in but give preference to families. Hurry up. We have no time to lose. Idle hands are a crime on this highway."

Suddenly, spotting Henry, he said, "You boy, come and give me a hand while evacuation is being done."

Henry came forward eager to help in any way he could with this towering personality.

He turned to Henry, saying, "Sanitize your hands. Thank God Sise brought my medical kit. This woman needs to be operated on right now or she will die. You hold my equipment and pass them to me."

Henry held the equipment and watched Bethune, the surgeon. Even in these primitive conditions, with his surgical gloves on, he made a neat cut on the swollen ulcer in her leg. His concentration was intense, and his hand steady.

Henry has been acquainted with the concept of God as a skilled surgeon, and now he is observing it firsthand. With a precise incision, the swollen area is opened, revealing a discharge of pus. Skilfully, he inserted his index finger into the swelling and created another small cut to extract an embedded piece of metal. The atheist, embodying a divine presence, softly mutters words that resemble a curse in the midst of this battle against pain and suffering. Henry stood alert, quietly handing over what the doctor required. After he had dressed the cut completely, he moved on to the next patient who required attention.

This continued for three days and nights. During the day, the hot sun blazed, threatening to burn everyone before it. The nights were cold. Most refugees had nothing to cover themselves with. The fortunate ones had a blanket, but it provided inadequate protection. Many of the refugees died not from enemy bullets but from hunger pangs and bad weather besides disease. Norman Bethune's eyes were bloodshot. He had hardly any rest or sleep. He drove himself and others too.

When he caught one of his subordinates sleeping for a long time, he awakened him with a prod saying, "This is no time to sleep. Get up, you lazy bones, and get back to work. There is so much to do for the sick and dying. We are here to help people; not to sleep ourselves."

The van made several trips, each time taking some more people. Every time Sise came, he had almost the same story to tell Norman Bethune. "I hammered at the door of the Governor's office and asked for vehicles. I made it clear that millions of people will lose their lives if they don't send anything. Even a car or primitive cart will do – anything to prevent people from walking miles and miles with bleeding feet."

"But the officials said they have nothing. Not even a motor car to lend them. In fact, nothing on wheels which I can spare, only what I have given you."

Bethune cursed, "The bloody incompetent people. Sise, just drive like hell, get the next lot away, and come back."

Sise made a record of sorts of the undefeatable human spirit as he was at the wheel for 48 hours, almost nonstop, ferrying people.

The day passed and night came. There was no food to be had. It was all finished. There was no food left for even Dr Bethune. He managed without complaining. He merely shrugged philosophically, "If half the people of Spain are starving, we can do so for a few hours as well. Not difficult."

Henry's stomach rumbled and he felt dizzy. Once again, he wondered about the insatiable energy of Norman Bethune who worked like a man possessed despite hunger pangs which he too must be feeling. A strange listlessness overcame Henry. His limbs felt heavy as if made of lead. He wanted to lie down and sleep. But he could not. He had to attend to the sick. The next day brought relief in the form of a hawker selling a cartful of oranges. A commonplace occurrence, except in the circumstances, he seemed unreal. No one knew from where he had come. They felt he had dropped straight from heaven. Norman Bethune hailed him, bought all his oranges, kept one for himself, and distributed the rest. The truck came back again and again. In the final round, Henry climbed abroad and reached Almeria along with his companions.

Worn out, they finally reached the outskirts of Almeria. An incredible sight met their eyes. Thousands and thousands of people, mostly wearing rags, swarmed the streets. The truck had to literally move at a crawling pace. The whole city seemed full of refugees. They swarmed everywhere, in the ports, on the roads and in the city square. They gazed at you with stricken eyes from the pavements. Finally, they reached the hospital premises, where everyone alighted. Henry wondered would the city burst from its seams. A tired Norman Bethune sat down on a cot and slept. Henry, too found a place to sleep.

At night, he was woken by the sound of wailing sirens. He jumped up only to hear the burst of explosions shattering everything before it. The explosions went on, one after another. Giant flames reared up, licking everything before them like firecrackers gone astray.

CHAPTER 14

Not content in going after the refugees on the highway, the Nationalists had bombed Almeria as well. Henry scrambled up and rubbed his sleepy eyes. Such was the intensity of the explosions one after another that the very cot he slept in seemed to shake, as did the bowels of the earth. If things went on the same way, the earth would be destroyed.

Stretcher in hand, Miguel and Henry ran as they heard a booming voice from the hospital, "Go to the centre of the city. That is where most people have been hit. Be quick. It may already be too late." The voice belonged to Norman Bethune.

One after another, the sound of explosions reached his ears. In the hospital premises, he could hear the sound of children screaming out of fright in the dormitory of the hospital they were housed in. Everywhere there was movement. People were running out. Henry could barely run in the sea of people. He was jostled at almost every few steps he went ahead. The planes continued to roar one after another. Screams rent the air. There were screams of agony and fright as the people did not know where the next bombs would drop. Sometimes, after long intervals, another sound came to Henry's ears – the *rat-a-tat* of anti-aircraft fire.

The heart of the city was completely devastated. Giant flames lit up the sky, enveloping even tall buildings which had once stood proud and erect. Most people had shocked and dazed expressions on their faces as they ran about, trying to escape from the rapidly crumbling walls of the huge buildings and scramble into bomb pits.

Henry tried to make his way to the wounded. It became very difficult though; he screamed, "Medico." He knew he could be hit as well. Then as suddenly as it started, the bombing stopped. The roar of aircraft engines overhead fell silent. Suddenly, a warm sight met his eyes. Amid ruin, Henry saw Norman Bethune carry a small whimpering girl about eight in his arms towards a waiting ambulance. He had himself rescued her from under a beam of a house, which had fallen. He had not waited for stretcher bearers but carried the girl herself, going out of his way to save lives.

Norman Bethune had always maintained, "The primary aim of a doctor is to save lives. Everything else is unimportant. If he cannot do that, then he is not a doctor worth his salt."

Norman Bethune was living up to his high ideals. He remained busy. Fortunately, now there were a few ambulances at his service.

Henry and Miguel, too, had no time to even think of themselves as they were carrying the wounded for treatment. Henry felt so tired that at one stage, he felt his limbs would give way and he would drop his stretcher. He wondered how Norman Bethune, a man decades older than him, could find the energy to keep working. He said so to Miguel.

Miguel said, "The man is superhuman. He hates the fascists, you know and he takes his role as a doctor seriously. It's the hatred for the fascists and his duty to the helpless people that drive him."

Henry came across a huge bomb crater right in the middle of the city. He turned away in horror. Inside it were bits and pieces of what had once been human clothing, broken pipes and parts of human flesh and bones ripped apart by the bombs. It was too gruesome a sight for any eyes. A wave of nausea overcame him. His stomach lurched. He turned to a side and retched, holding the sides of his abdomen. A sticky liquid came out. It was bile. There was hardly anything in his stomach to come out. He had not eaten for the last twelve hours. Miguel was by his side, offering him miraculously a bottle of water. Henry did not know how he had managed it.

Miguel asked, "Do you want to take a breather?"

Henry shook his head, "No, I am alright."

They continued to work. To his surprise, he found the old man in one of the collapsed houses. He had a bottle of whiskey in his hand. It was the same old man who had talked with him at length on the Malaga-Almeria highway.

He recognized Henry, "Still at it, laddie. See, the bombs fell, but I survived again."

Henry smiled, "You are a born survivor."

The old man shook his head, "Don't want to be one. I wanted to die, but nothing ever kills me. What is a useless old man like me doing in this world?"

Henry held up his hand, "Don't speak like this."

The old man said, "It's the young who deserve to live. You have plenty of work in front of you. Everywhere people who are needed are dying and useless people like me are spared and forced to live, people who have nobody to mourn them – who have nothing to live for."

"You are depressed because of the times we live in. Maybe, you would not have felt the same way in better times."

"Better times. Yes, I have seen those as well. There was a time when I had a family. We even had some land to farm. It was the days before the Great Depression. Spain was then full of olive groves that brought money, and so did bullfighting. Seville, which is now in Franco's hands, was full of orange trees. Oranges were littering the streets. Thousands of them just fell down, making a carpet of oranges. Their heady fragrance filled the air. In those days, hunger was not common. At that time, the desire to live was strong. You see, I had a family to care for. All I needed was a bit of money and pals to drink with. Even then, I loved my drink. This is the only love I have retained. We were never rich or even middle class but we pulled through. Politically, we were never a democracy. We always veered towards autocracy. This time, there was a chance, but we seem to be losing it. Its sheer military power that is our undoing and the rise of Franco."

Henry muttered, "It always comes back to Franco."

"Yes, he believes in Conservatism. He belonged to a military family. So, I guess it was natural to go into the army. Power went to his head. He rose too fast. He was Brigadier General at the age of 33 in Morocco. It was there that he proved his military acumen. He saw his chance in the 1936 coup and seized it with both hands."

Henry nodded.

The old man continued, "It's the lust for power. I don't have an iota of faith in what many misguided people believe that he is fighting for his ideals like anti-communism. He is simply after power and somehow, I feel that soon, he will get his way."

Henry said, "It will be a sad day in history if he does so."

"It is already terrible. The fascists have lost all sense of humanity. They could have gone after us at places of strategic military positions like the port. But they concentrated on human flesh. They knew that the people in Almeria were from Malaga and look at the way they have butchered them. It is all Spanish blood that has been spilt on the streets, and they do not care an iota for them. Women and children have lost their lives. People have been maimed for life, forced to live a life worse than death. How can they be so cruel and short-sighted? It is Spanish people they will need when they come to power. Don't they realize that people in general, will be bitter and refuse to cooperate? Memories are long and personal loss of family members can never be forgotten."

Henry said vehemently, "They have lost all logic. Even other countries who are sitting on the fence do not realize the gravity of the situation."

The old man nodded, "This is the reality of life. You may watch others dig their graves like silent spectators but not know when you fall into them yourselves. This is what those neutral countries are doing, watching Spain bleed from the sidelines without rushing to its help. There is bound to be a World War which will take the world to the jaws of hell."

Henry said, "Humanity is not totally lost. There is a man like Norman Bethune who works day and night. He lives up to the Hippocratic Oath, '*Into whatsoever house I enter; there shall I heal the sick…*' The difference is that this time, it is not just a house but an entire city whose people need healing."

The old man nodded, "Yes, there is suffering everywhere without a few parallels in history. There are a few people in the stature of Norman Bethune with the ability, intelligence and resources to help others revive. But it is not only Norman Bethune who is helping Spain. Each and every member who volunteered to join the International Brigade is doing so as well. Why, you are not rendering any less service than Norman Bethune. You have displayed immense patience in listening to the ramblings of an old man. Just talking to you has made me feel better."

Henry thanked the old man and was about to bid him goodbye when he said, "So many in the International Brigades have made the supreme sacrifice."

The image of a carefree Robert came to Henry's mind. He wondered at the grief inflicted on his parents. He may never know. He would only find out when he reached Madrid, but at present, he had to work here to bring relief.

CHAPTER 15

Henry returned to Madrid after two days. On the way back, there was only one topic of discussion everywhere – the fall of Malaga and the brutal bombing of the people.

A man on the road said, "Shame on the Republicans for not fighting back. They did not put up a semblance of a fight not even proper rearguard action. The men from the International Brigades did fight but not the armed forces of the government. Their attempt to save people was negligible. They let Malaga fall into Nationalist hands on a platter. Now, you can be sure that it is Franco who will win and come to power. The Republicans are losing and retribution that follows when Franco assumes total control of Spain will be terrible."

Henry was silent. What could he say?

"I have heard they have already jailed and tortured all Republican supporters, even members of the International Brigade. Many have been shot dead. Their only crime is supporting the government. The Nationalists are a sadistic lot. Just wait until they win and we will know the true extent of their cruelty."

Henry said, "The people of Spain have suffered enough. Their cities have been bombed to almost ruins. Most of them have known the death of their family members. Millions have been rendered homeless. Thousands have died of starvation and disease. What more can they suffer?"

The cynical man said, "Wait and watch. I feel the worst is yet to come. There will be a bloodbath." He left after saying these foreboding words.

He reached Madrid at dusk. The sun had already set. Most of the streets were deserted except for a few people. The lights remained dimmed. The debris of once proud buildings was all over the roads, especially the working-class quarters. It was a city reeling under suffering, ruined and tattered but still fighting, waiting for the final onslaught.

There was a letter from Edwina, which was handed over to Henry. It had come a few days back. Henry tore it open. It was written in Edwina's neat handwriting but was blurred in places. It was evident that tears had fallen even while she was writing.

'Dear Henry,

I can't get over the shock and grief of Robert's death. There are days when I feel very low. [The next few lines were smudged.] But no matter how I feel, I know his parents will feel worse. I could not bear to give them the news through a letter.

I took a train and went to Hampshire. I could locate the house. It was one of those typical double-storied English cottages with a front garden where there was a bed of roses. I felt my heart break the moment I caught sight of it. It looked like such a serene house where life went about almost the same way day after day. There was no hint of even the edge of a war cloud. The life of the English countryside remained in full splendour. Here, I had come to break what must be devastating news and shatter the calm forever. If I, as a close friend, found it so difficult to bear it, how could they who had given birth and reared him?

I knocked at the wooden door. The door was opened by what looked like a maid. The maid looked at me inquisitively, wondering what my purpose was. I introduced myself as Robert's friend and then I was let in and taken to what appeared to be a living room. Both Robert's parents were at home. His mother wearing a bright blue floral printed frock, came into the room with eager extended hands, her lips beginning to curl in a smile of greeting which faded when she looked at my pale face. Something in my expression may have given me away. His father, a grey-haired man with piercing blue eyes, said at once, "It's bad news."

I nodded and simply broke the news. His mother just collapsed. His father took the blow better but sat down with a bewildered and lost look on his face. He simply said, "God help us. He was our only son. All we have now is our daughter."

When he used the past tense, I realized he had accepted that his son was dead.

Much later, I showed them your letter with details of Robert's death. In the evening, I left them to their grief. There was no way I could console them. What could I say? What can anyone say to parents who have lost their child? It is, perhaps, one of the greatest tragedies of life. I will never forget the expression on their faces for the rest of my life. It will haunt me forever.

Henry, do take care of yourself. I hardly get any news of what is happening in Spain except through newspaper columns. I want to see you return to England whole and sound. [She had underlined the next words.] Do not take unnecessary risks. I will write again. I cannot write any further today, or I'll completely break down.'

Henry read the letter twice. A few tears escaped his eyes for what once was and can never be again. Everything in the past seemed gone and life was so different. Even if he went back, he thought the old life would not return. The carefree days were gone forever. Besides, he had Rosa to think of.

He had heard that Norman Bethune, too, was back in Madrid. It was Miguel who gave him the news. "I have heard that Norman Bethune is back. He is even more angry and loses his temper often. He just can't stand the red tape of the bureaucracy which prevents him from taking quick action. He is at loggerheads with the Spanish authorities. A doc I talked to said he is blasting them left, right and centre and losing it. But once he is at the front looking after the wounded, he is a different man. He never loses his cool then. He is the epitome of care and compassion. He is equally rational. He acts fast and his methods certainly work. Thousands of patients breathe better because of him. Those who have seen him can vouch for it."

Henry murmured, "I can believe that."

He found his footsteps going towards the main city shops hoping to catch a glimpse of Rosa. It was an idle dream.

He did not even know if he would ever see her again. It seemed an unlikely prospect. Despite so much happening, Robert's death and the tragedy he had witnessed had not changed his thoughts or feelings for her. Rosa had become his secret obsession which he could not overcome.

It happened then. From a distance, he could make out that it was Rosa he saw. He could, he thought, smell her from a distance. It was Rosa at a shop, but somehow, she looked different. She had a crimson skirt ending just below her knees and a flowery patterned top with large bold flowers. Her red hair, which fell loose over her shoulders, shimmered. As Henry came closer, he saw that she wore lipstick. What was worse, Rosa was not alone. There was a man with her and she was leaning on him while he had his arm around her shoulders. Henry looked on stupefied. There was a smile on Rosa's face. It was a different smile from what she gave him. A more inviting, tantalizing smile – the smile of a lover for her beloved. Her eyes, too, seemed to melt. She had never looked so beautiful before.

Henry stood dumbstruck. It was obvious that Rosa was with the man she loved. She had never given him such smiles. It was so different from the one she gave him. He realized it was a warm, friendly smile, but he realized that was all she felt. He closed his eyes. He wanted to turn his back and run away; anything to avoid seeing her. But something, he knew not what, propelled him forward. He found his footsteps going towards Rosa. It was perhaps the devil prompting him. He knew what he had seen with his eyes could not be wrong. Yet, something prompted him to hear her voice – to confirm by her voice one last time.

He knew that such a confirmation would only cause him more distress. He went towards Rosa. His only prayer was that he would not betray himself.

He found that he could say nonchalantly, pretending an air of surprise, "Rosa! What a surprise."

She spun around, exclaiming, "Henry. How are you?'

There was genuine concern in her voice. Henry said in a light voice, "I am ok. Nothing damaged."

The man beside Rosa turned. Henry could see a tall man with blond hair and a trimmed beard.

He said, "Rosa, you have not introduced us."

Rosa said, "How bad of me. I seem to have forgotten the basic courtesies. This is Henry, whom we brought home from the front. I told you about him. Henry, this is Bert, my neighbour. I have some good news. We are engaged to be married perhaps in a short while."

Henry wondered later how he managed it. He felt like collapsing to the ground as he heard the shattering news. But he kept his voice steady and managed a smile while extending his hand, "Congratulations. This is great. But I must be leaving you now. There is work to be done."

He turned around and walked away without looking back. He felt that a knife had been driven into his being, twisting it inside. He felt suddenly short of breath, as if suffocating. The fact kept resounding in his brain, '*Rosa does not love me. She loves someone else. She cares for someone else.*' A feeling of emptiness gripped him. His body felt hollow all over. He was dry-eyed but in agony. He knew that the loss and grief he felt was now intense but its edges would dull with time. Time was supposed to heal everything, wasn't it? He did not know the answer as he walked away, his footsteps going like a robot.

CHAPTER 16

Miguel was the first to perceive that something was wrong with Henry. He seemed listless, going about his work in a mechanical manner. There was a marked lack of enthusiasm. His long face and sad eyes told Miguel that something was seriously wrong. It could be bad news from home or a broken heart. The latter was more likely. If there was bad news from home, he would have shared it.

When he had time, he asked, "It's Rosa, is it not?"

Henry looked up. He hated sharing the secrets of his innermost heart with anyone, even old faithful Miguel. All he could do was nod. Miguel thought it better to leave him alone. He did not question him further. All he said was, "You want to share it with me?"

Henry shook his head. He did not feel like talking at all. Miguel did not probe any further. He said, "Whatever it is, you will overcome. We all do so. We have to go to the front today. There have been many casualties."

Henry hurried along. Miguel's urgency told him that there was no time to lose. He could not afford to wallow in heartbreak. In a way, he was glad. He desperately wanted something to take his mind off his own troubled heart. Work, perhaps, was the best panacea. The front was in the dusty hillside. Vast clouds of dust bellowed out beside smoke from shells. Everything seemed covered in a generous coat of dust, including artillery guns. Soldiers, too, wore it with only the slits of their eyes visible.

While ferrying the wounded to safety, Henry saw a strange sight. He saw a woman and a man with cameras in their hands, clicking pictures of the action. Bullets whizzed past them but they did not seem to bother. It was the first time that Henry had seen a woman so close to the front. She was busy clicking pictures and recording whatever she saw. Her name, he was to learn later, was Gerda Taro. Dressed in a shirt and pants, her intense look of concentration made him realise that she was concentrating only on the action, braving discomfort and the danger of death. Her companion was Robert Capa. What Henry did not know was that the Spanish Civil War was perhaps the first conflict in which photographers managed to capture the action from close quarters, which became a sort of trendsetter. Robert Capa would become one of the most famous war journalists of the twentieth century. He was right in the heart of battles in the Second World War as well. However, these events would occur only in the future. At present, he was a combat photographer who maintained that unless photographs were shot from up close, they were of no use and people would not be able to understand what was happening in the combat field. His iconic picture, *The Falling Soldier*, captured a Republican soldier falling at the moment of his death in the Spanish Civil War in a trench in Andalusia, Spain.

Commenting on the photograph, he said later, "This thing repeated itself about three or four times, so the fourth time I just kind of put my camera above my head and even didn't look and clicked a picture when they moved over the trench. And that was all. I didn't ever look at my pictures there and I sent my pictures back with a lot of other pictures that I took."

These photographers and journalists took as much risk as the soldiers. Many of them died in action. Henry later learned that Greda and Robert formed a team of sorts. They had a professional association. The gossip went that Robert was in love with Greda, who had rebuffed him. However, they continued their professional journey.

Henry saw another man who was noting down all events. He was dressed in khakis, a casual corduroy jacket and sturdy boots. He was so engrossed in his task that he did not see a bullet whizz past almost near him. Henry, who standing near, forced him to lie down at once. He peered at the man. He was a large man with a rugged, sun-tanned face and a huge moustache.

He said, "Thanks, boy. You have saved my life."

Henry answered, "Don't thank me. It was a chance that I was there and noticed the bullet in time. May I give you some advice? Do not get close to the line of action. It could be dangerous."

The man laughed, "Flirting with danger is an old habit. I don't die easily. You are doing so, too, and you don't look like a Spaniard to me."

"You are right. I am a stretcher bearer, so I am simply doing my job. I belong to the International Brigade."

"Ah, I worked for the Red Cross in World War I – an ambulance driver. We have something in common. What's your name?"

"Henry. I am from England."

"Well, I am Earnest Hemmingway from the US."

Henry looked awestruck. He was in the presence of the great Hemmingway – a novelist and journalist. What would Edwina say to this fact? Would Rosa know? Then, he brushed that thought out of his mind. Why couldn't he let go of Rosa? He should only concentrate on the present.

Henry could not help saying, "Despite these unusual circumstances in which we have met, let me say that I have read *A Farewell to Arms* – a great work indeed. I borrowed it from the library."

"Ah, so you love reading?"

"Yes, I do. I am also a student of English Literature. Let me boldly say that you have a unique writing style and understand the economy of words."

Hemmingway nodded. And then, asked a question which took Henry by surprise, "Look here, I am sure you are staying somewhere nearby. Maybe Madrid?"

Henry nodded.

"Then, why don't you meet me for dinner at the Florida hotel? I am putting up there. Food and drinks are still available there. The crockery is good too. If I know anything about wars I doubt if you have sat down on a table with proper crockery to have a meal. It's poor repayment for the task you have done, but at present, it will have to suffice."

Henry saw at once that he was in the presence of a great personality, "I'll be glad to join you."

That night when he was free, Henry dressed with care. He wore the best clothes he carried, which were cleaned, washed and ironed. He combed his hair.

Miguel said, "Lucky you. You are sure to get good drinks and a fine dinner. I have gathered some information about this Hemmingway of yours. He loves his drink and is going around with Martha Gellhorn, another bold woman correspondent. He is, I believe, married. If you are lucky, you will catch a glimpse of her. She flouts convention and wears real short skirts. Her slim legs are a sight for a man's eyes."

"This is all gossip. Anyway, what matters is that I am having dinner with a writer and a war correspondent to boot."

"Writers are not unique here. Madrid is full of them."

Hotel Florida was situated in Central Madrid in Callao Square. The hotel itself, with its ten stories and its square-shaped marble façade, was an inspiring sight. At night, it had all its lights on and glittered like an isolated jewel. Sounds of gay laughter drifted from inside. The hotel, Henry had learnt, had two hundred rooms with attached bathrooms. During the war, the hotel was home to several foreign correspondents, writers, intellectuals and artists – all who supported the Republican cause.

Standing outside the hotel, Henry wondered if Hemmingway was true to his words. He was. The moment he entered the dining room, Hemmingway extended his arms to welcome him. He had changed into a dinner jacket. A discreet waiter ushered them to a table.

Hemmingway said, “Ah, here we can talk,” ordering drinks. He turned to Henry and asked, “Why are you here?”

Henry answered, “It’s where my duty lay.” He found himself talking about Robert and Edwina and how he volunteered.

“This is your first time in Spain?”

Henry nodded. “Not yours, I guess. Your works suggest you are familiar with it.”

Hemmingway laughed, “Oh, yes. I am an old-timer. I have always loved Spain. It’s the country that I loved more than any other except my own,” It’s a pity that it has been hit by tragedy. I am an aficionado of the sport of bullfighting. I have been to Spain several times when perhaps you were a schoolboy and saw bullfights. I knew many matadors. You may have read *Death in the Afternoon*.”

Henry answered, “Unfortunately not.”

“Ah, then you have missed something. Try to get hold of it. I am quoting what I feel and have said countless times. Bullfighting is the only art in which the artist is in danger of death and in which the degree of brilliance in the performance is left to the fighter’s honour. Only a few sports on this earth invite danger – where a man’s life is at risk, like motor racing and mountaineering. I love hunting, including big game, because of the scent of danger. I am a good shot. The rest is all fun and games. I’ve taken risks all my life. I wouldn’t be here if I weren’t.”

Henry nodded, "Being in the combat zone, you face as much danger as any soldier."

"Yeah. But that's what I like. You must know why I joined the war. The tearing of Spain by the fascists is too much to bear. It is not only people who are suffering. Entire cities have been reduced to rubble. Art work which has withstood the onslaught of a thousand centuries is now destroyed. Franco is aided by the people I hate: Hitler and Mussolini. I was in Germany in the twenties. I saw the economic and social hardships that people had to suffer. The situation was just right for an unscrupulous politician like Hitler to take centre stage. I was also one of the first to interview that jerk, Mussolini. He is the biggest bluff in Europe and now, he has come to aid another jerk, Franco. If Franco comes to power, democracy will be wiped out. Spanish people will lose their basic liberty – the right of choice. My conscience told me that this was the time to stop Hitler, or we would have another World War on our hands. A hell-broth is brewing and it is bound to spill over. I am a man who loves action. Once I knew that Spain was suffering, I came here. Of course, I work. I am reporting for the North American Newspaper Alliance (NANA). I have a typewriter in my room."

"You have a long association with Spain."

"I am attached to this country. I first visited Spain in 1923. At that time, I was putting up in Paris. It was bullfighting which drew me. Spain is also culturally rich."

A few partridges were served.

Hemmingway said, "We are in luck. I got a few partridges today morning. Shot them, I mean."

Henry looked awestruck. '*Was there nothing this man could not do?*

Henry asked hesitatingly, "Are you working on another novel?"

Hemmingway smiled, "I am trying my hand at playwriting. Let's see what comes out. I am also working on the film – The Spanish Earth. Both are based on what we are seeing on the ground. I feel that people like you and I cannot change the tide of war. Franco will win. The Republicans continue to be a disorganized lot. I can foresee another World War where these countries who are now neutral will be sucked in, maybe my country as well."

CHAPTER 17

The words sounded like a prophecy. Hemmingway continued, "I have been closely watching Europe's political developments and the rise of Nazism. I know the evils it stands for. I have warned the world through my writings and newspaper columns, but they still think Hitler can be controlled through appeasement. If we can't stop Hitler now, which I feel we are unlikely to do, we will face devastation. He is going from strength to strength. I am sure that the Second World War is just around the corner. Hitler's appetite will not be satisfied with crumbs. He will want to gobble up the entire Europe. The war will be the bloodiest we have seen yet. Mark my words."

Someone called out, "Earnest, we are waiting for you." It was a woman's voice.

He rose from the table. Hemmingway said, "I must leave." He shook hands with Henry. He said as a parting shot, "If you want to meet me, you will most probably find me here."

Henry described the meeting to Miguel, who was agog with curiosity. At length, he said, "Well, I have gathered some news for you as well. I know you will be interested. It is about Norman Bethune."

"Ah, what's the latest? He is here in Madrid, isn't he?"

"No. He is in Barcelona. Remember his conversation about establishing villages for war children? Well, after days of pestering the government authorities to give the nod, they finally have."

"Where will he set them up?"

"In Barcelona. The Northern Industrial Metropolis. It's a relatively quiet place, comparatively remote from fighting and bombing. Therefore, the location is ideal for keeping these orphaned children in children's villages."

Henry whistled, "The idea is superb and innovative, just like Norman Bethune but from where will he get funds?"

"The Spanish Aid Committee in Toronto. Bethune has appealed to them to raise money for the project. They have agreed. He wants to set up a chain of children's villages. I believe two will be set up finally."

Henry said, "That's good news."

"Yes, these war orphans will be taken care of. I have heard that nothing touches Bethune's heart as much as children."

"There is a lot he has already done."

Miguel answered, "Yes. He is a hero to many people, but there are others who just can't stand him. He is outspoken. The Spanish doctors working with him do not like him. They think he is too ambitious and overbearing. The military officials and other bureaucrats have a hard time with him. He does lose his temper often and blasts them. The feeling is that he acts too big for his boots and wants to control the Institute, which they don't like."

Henry said, "But his work speaks for itself."

Miguel shook his head sadly, "Sometimes, work is not enough. Other things matter which have little to do with your profession."

There was a call from outside. "We have to head for Guadalajara. There have been casualties. It was an Italian offensive. Hurry up. The truck is waiting to take us."

Henry and Miguel were on their feet and quickly threw a few things in their knapsack, including tinned food. They ran out and climbed on board the waiting truck.

Darkness had descended, and the tall trees cast eerie shadows against the moonlight. A cold wind was blowing. Henry turned up the collar of his jacket beneath his blue overalls.

As they were on the road, another medical man said, "The Nationalists launched this operation out of frustration. They lost the battle of Jarama and have so far failed to capture Madrid. Now, the Italians have taken charge. Mussolini has, I believe, given the go-ahead. The Spanish Nationalists forces are there but they hardly count. It is the Italians who are spearheading the attack and calling all the shots."

Henry said, "Where are they concentrating? We will have to reach where the actual action is taking place."

"The real offensive has begun in the 25 km-wide pass at Guadalajara-Alcalá de Henares. There are, I believe, five roads there, with three of them leading to the city which they want to capture."

"Then, they must have come with a huge army."

"Yes. You are right. They have about 35,000 soldiers, tankettes, armoured vehicles, etc. They even have air support. It's a pretty enviable position."

Henry asked, "And we?"

"Not too good. Just the 12th Division of the People's Republican Army. Colonel Lacalle is in charge. He has just one company of light tanks and a mere ten thousand soldiers. He is outnumbered in every way. The Republicans have also been unable to build solid defence positions."

"Then, we are in for an agonizing time with plenty of casualties."

When they arrived after a bumpy ride, the fascists had already advanced and the Republicans were retreating. Bodies of the dead and the wounded were strewn everywhere. Henry remained busy picking up the wounded and shifting them to waiting ambulances. The Republicans, he believed, had called for more reinforcements. They had one silver lining. The weather seemed to favour them as fog descended and visibility was low. Henry and other stretcher bearers had trouble wading through sleet and fog to pick up the wounded. Some of them lost their footing and were seriously hurt. The poor weather continued through the next day. The Nationalists were advancing, though slowly, capturing territory and towns. The IX International Brigades fought for the Republicans and managed to repulse the attack. A couple of days later, the Republican forces launched an effective counter-attack. The International Brigade successfully began to advance.

There was panic among the Italians who retreated. A wave of confidence enveloped the Republicans. The Republicans finally managed to recapture the cities of Guadalajara and Villaviciosa de Tajuña. It was a great strategic victory. It put a temporary end to the encirclement of Madrid and its eventual fall. Henry was there for almost a week helping the sick and the wounded. Some of them were transported to better hospitals through hospital trains.

CHAPTER 18

The victory was a morale booster for the Republicans, who were now more confident. Henry now received further news of Norman Bethune.

He heard from one of the doctors at the hospital, "Norman Bethune is full of plans. This victory seems to have geared him up. He wants to do more daring experiments where blood is concerned and spread his network throughout the country."

Henry also got a chance to work closely with the great man. He felt in awe of him but he could easily perceive that he was not a man to suffer fools gladly. He heard him shouting, "What do these bloody Spanish officials know about blood or the sick? They do not have a medical degree. Why should they poke their noses into what is none of their business? The Republican army officials are the worst. Their noses are too long. Even when they don't bloody well understand the ABC of medical science, they must interfere. I just cannot stand them."

Later, Henry found him arguing with a senior official, raising his voice to a higher pitch. "What the bloody hell do you mean stopping me? My duty lies in saving lives and let me do it my way. The Institute cannot be run by people whose job is to command the armed forces. Anyway, I feel you are doing a bad job of that as well."

The red-faced official said, "How I lead my forces is none of your concern. The trouble is you are not acquainted with the Spanish language and our ways. This is not Canada; you've got to follow the rules. We are not interfering with your work but help to guide you and run the administration. You are here to help us but not run things."

Bethune was now screaming. His face had gone purple, "You will teach me how to run an Institute after everything I have done? I am trying to bloody help you run the show. It's not you I care about but the suffering and helpless Spanish people. I want to reach out to as many people as possible. So, we are expanding our network. I am arranging funds as well. Where do you think the dole is coming from? We have given life to thousands. But red tape and rules cannot be allowed to come in the way of treatment. Anyone in a critical condition needs help at that moment; not even a second to lose. I am sick and tired of explaining such things to you all. You all are so selfish that you do not care for your own people."

The red-faced official retorted, "If we didn't care for people, you wouldn't be here. Don't forget you are on foreign soil."

Bethune's voice rose to dangerous levels, "Are you threatening me? I will report at once to your superior."

The Spanish official cooled down a bit, "Of course not. I have no right to."

A doctor who had also overheard the spat said, "The trouble with Norman Bethune for all his good qualities is that he seems to rub people the wrong way. His ability to communicate effectively and get along with people is not good. He loses his temper often. A good leader should know how to carry his team with him, whatever nationality they may belong to."

Henry said, "Whatever issues there may be, I have seen him at work. I've yet to see a man who espouses the cause of humanity so fervently. I have seen him rescue children from ruins and carry refugees to safety in ambulances. Besides, he is a dedicated and highly innovative doctor."

"What you say is true, but there is the other side. In Spain, people do not like a doctor with Bethune's lifestyle. A section in the military feels his moral conduct is wanting."

"But has moral conduct or whatever you call it have anything to do with his work? You cannot dictate to a man about his personal life. That's strictly his own business."

"It may apply to any ordinary person, maybe. But they feel it is important when he is holding a position of authority. As you know, he is a heavy drinker and the woman in his life exerts an undue interference at the institute. He seems to let her, and this is causing trouble. Then, there is this temper of his which he seems unable to control. Wait and see how things play out. I can't help feeling that his days in Spain are numbered."

Henry said, "It is a pity if things happen that way. He has already done so much for the Spanish Cause."

Unfortunately, the Spanish doctor's words proved to be prophetic. It happened while Henry was working in the same hospital as Bethune. The landline telephone rang.

Henry, who happened to be near the instrument, picked up the phone.

A voice at the other end said in clipped, polite tones, "Is Norman Bethune there? I would like to talk to him."

Henry said, "I'll try to find him."

The voice had a ring of authority, "You better be quick, boy. Don't keep me waiting."

Henry ran and shouted, "Someone, please call Norman Bethune. There is a call for him."

Norman Bethune hurried down the stairs, "Who the devil has called me now?"

He answered, "Hello. Yes, this is Norman Bethune speaking. What do you want?'

Henry overheard Bethune saying, "I don't know what your opinion is about the degree of importance, but I feel the first priority is to save lives, Mr Carlos Contreras."

The man at the other end spoke for ten minutes and at last, Bethune heaving an exasperated sigh, said, "Ok, I'll be there at the appointed time and then we can discuss."

Norman Bethune returned the receiver to the holder and said, "These crazy Spaniards."

Henry later asked another Spanish doctor, "I wonder who is Carlos Contreras?"

The Spanish doctor said, "He is the leader of the Fifth Regiment. He is very influential. His word carries weight as it has government backing."

After a few days, it was Miguel who broke the news. He said with sadness, "I have news that you will not like. Norman Bethune is leaving Spain."

Henry looked at him aghast. "Why? There is so much to do here!"

"You remember you told me about his meeting with Carlos Contreras. Well, this is what transpired at the meeting."

"Do you know what happened?"

"Not really, but I can take you to someone who has inside knowledge. He can tell us more."

Henry said, "Then, do so."

Miguel introduced him to a Canadian doctor who worked in Bethune's unit. He did not seem to be too disheartened. In a calm and composed manner, he answered Henry, who asked him, "Yes, it is true. Norman Bethune will soon leave Spain. He was frustrated when he heard the news but he accepted it later."

"You mean they actually fired him in a way?"

The Canadian looked shocked, "They can't do that. He is his own master."

"Was it the outcome of the meeting with Carlos Contreras?"

"Well, yes. They did not spell out in words that he was not needed here. They suggested that he do some other important work and Carlos was very convincing. Bethune later told us that Carlos had said that the recent victory had upped the morale of the Republicans. He felt the fascists could be defeated. What was needed was weapons and money. True, the Soviet Union was doing its best and giving military equipment and arms, but the Italians attacked and sunk even those unarmed ships carrying weapons. France, Britain and the US had refused to supply them with arms maintaining their position of neutrality. Norman Bethune had been in Spain for some time. Being a well-known personality, he could go on a lecture tour in North America and put the Spanish cause and the plight of its people before the people of North America. North American aid in the form of money and arms could save the Republic from destruction. This, they thought, as the blood transfusion unit was running pretty smoothly and could take care of itself, leaving him free for more important work. They felt it was the need of the hour and only Bethune could do it."

"What was Bethune's reaction?"

"He did not like it in the beginning. The war, he felt, was far from over and there was a lot more he could do for the suffering people. He had made many plans and intended to carry them out. But he was forced to concede to the logic of the arguments. He decided to discuss it with his Canadian colleagues at the Institute. They seem to agree with Contreras. They, too, felt that there was an urgent need for Bethune to go on a lecture tour and influence North America to contribute to the war. Well, Bethune has finally agreed."

CHAPTER 19

Henry felt bad. He thought that the Republicans were making a mistake in sending away their truest friend who, although blunt in his ways, had devoted his life to taking care of people. Henry felt that it was doubtful that the United States would have a sudden change of heart and jump into the fray. Besides, it was struggling with its problems at home.

Bethune winded up his affairs slowly. He thought that there was an unfinished job left. A Canadian literary magazine, *Hew Frontier*, had requested him for an article on Spain. He decided to write in Madrid while he was still in the thick of things. From it burst forth "An Apology for Not Writing Letters." The film Heart of Spain, showcasing his work in Spain and the Spanish people's grave plight, was also ready. Bethune intended to screen the documentary on his lecture tours.

Soon, the time to leave had come. A farewell ceremony was organized by the Institute. Spanish officials also attended. They were generous in their praise and admitted that Bethune's work, especially in blood transfusion right on the front, reduced mortality by almost seventy-five per cent.

Bethune left Spain on June 6, 1937. Henry felt a lump in his throat when he heard that he had left. He could not help feeling that Spain would be much poorer with his departure. He was a man of immense stature and dedication. Suddenly, Henry had a surreal feeling. He felt in his bones that this was not the last he had seen or heard of Henry Bethune; he would see more of him, how and when, he did not know.

Meanwhile, life had to go on. Rosa's image did come into his mind repeatedly, but he brushed it aside. There was a strange feeling of hollowness inside him, which he tried to ignore. What was the use of thinking about what he could not have? It was better to concentrate only on the work at hand. It was Miguel who noticed Henry's changing expressions. He had come to know him so well. Miguel, the remarkable man from Italy known as *El Hombre de Italia.* Henry crossed paths with him when they both served as stretcher bearers, and from the moment they met, Miguel exuded an air of confidence. His wealth of experience traces back to his homeland, where he made the bold decision to leave upon Mussolini's rise to power. Seeking refuge in Switzerland, Miguel's journey eventually led him to Spain, where he joined the International Brigade to support the Republican cause. Throughout their time together, Miguel proved to be an unwavering presence for Henry, standing by him through every challenge they faced. Henry couldn't help but wonder if Miguel had been specially sent to lend an ear to his concerns and help find solutions. It seemed as though Miguel himself had no worries, as he fully embraced the philosophy that life is meant to be lived and ardently pursued the noble cause they fought for.

He patted Henry's back, saying, "Don't think of her. A few more months and you will get over it. As someone said, nothing is permanent."

Henry smiled and gushed, "Oh, Miguel, what will I do without you? I hope we never part." He gave Miguel a tight squeeze.

"Don't be so emotional. We are in this war together. Even when it is over, we will keep in touch."

A lot had happened since Bethune's departure. The Nationalists were slowly but steadily advancing. There would be prolonged periods of lull when nothing seemed to happen with bursts of Nationalist advance. Bilbao fell and so did countless small towns. The Aragon offensive by the Nationalists was a success. The Republicans faced disaster. With time, it became apparent that the Nationalists would win.

As the months passed, Miguel said, "Wait, it is the turn of Catalonia next. The Nationalists are advancing towards it."

Henry said, "At this pace, the war will be over within months. But I have to leave. The order has just arrived. I have to proceed towards Gandesa to help the XV International Brigade."

"All the best and take care. I have been directed to go to Ebro."

The Nationalists who were advancing had reached the outskirts of the city of Gandesa. The International Brigade were trying to stop their advance and hold on to the city. Spring was in the air. A light breeze was blowing while the naked branches of the trees were dressed in new leaves.

Henry was busy carrying wounded soldiers to a hospital in the city. His partner was another stretcher bearer, Herbert. He said, "There is another man who looks a little different although he is a Britisher like you. Everyone thinks he is an Iraqi although he claims otherwise."

"What's his name? Do I know him?"

"You are not likely to. You have not been with this regiment before. His name is John Smith."

The name rang a bell. He had heard of him somewhere though at that moment he could not recall where. He was soon to meet him. As he was relaxing with a cigarette under the shade of an ancient oak, he spotted another man with a small moustache and large black eyes in a deeply tanned nut-brown face donning the uniform of a soldier of the International Brigade. Henry stared at him. He looked like an Indian; it was a rare sight as there were so few Indians in the International Brigade. He had met only a doctor so far. Henry approached the man, who stared back at him with a questioning look. Henry was the first to break the ice.

He said, extending his hand, "I am Henry and you guessed right, if I am not mistaken. I am half Indian."

The man smiled broadly, holding his hand. "I am John Smith from the British Battalion."

Henry frowned but smiled back. "I, too, come from England. I live there."

The man called John Smith said, "Are you off duty?"

Henry answered, "At present."

"Then let us go to a café, I know. It is pretty nearby. We can talk there."

Henry walked into the café with the man called John Smith. They ordered drinks and sandwiches. As they relaxed, the man asked, "Your lineage interests me. Is your father an Indian?"

"No, my mother is. I have travelled to India off and on. My nanaji lives there."

The man smiled and said, "Then, you must have guessed my lineage too."

Henry merely smiled.

The man said, "My real name is not John Smith. It is Gopal Mukund Huddar. John Smith is a name I gave myself. It's a common name which I picked at random. I somehow did not want to reveal my real identity. However, one fact is true. I was living in England when I joined."

Henry asked, very interested, "Were you brought up there?"

Huddar shook his head, "No. I was born in Madhya Pradesh and brought up in Nagpur. I had my education there. I received my graduate degree from Morris College. Right from my early days, I wanted to drive away the British from India. The atmosphere in the country was such that almost everyone was gripped with patriotic fervour. We wanted to live in an independent India."

"I know something about it. My nanaji's family are staunch patriots. They are great fans of Gandhiji and Nehru."

"Most people are. I have my differences with their viewpoint, especially their belief in non-violence. I believe any means can be adopted to drive them out."

"Then, you must have been interested in politics from an early age."

"Yes. I joined a secret society called *Rashtriya Swayam Sevak Sangh* (RSS). I was even made its General Secretary. I was only 23 then. However, my stint there was not very fruitful. I found that it was all about delving into and promoting Hindu Civilization. There was very little revolutionary fervour in it. I wanted to free my motherland from colonial rule, even if it meant breaking the law. I was not scared of imprisonment or even death in those days. I was imprisoned and served a jail sentence."

Henry asked, "What was your offence?"

Huddar smiled ruefully, "I stole arms and was caught."

Henry asked, his eyebrow raised, "Then?"

"Jail was not bad. I read and wrote a lot. I came in contact with people who wanted the same goals; other freedom fighters. Of course, I lost my freedom."

Henry leaned forward and asked, "Then?"

"I was released in 1935. So, I spent about four years in jail. By that time, I was no longer in the RSS. I believed in the ideology of the left."

Henry whistled, "Then, you are a true freedom fighter. How did you land up in England?"

"I didn't have the money, but I had true friends. A philanthropist and other friends made it possible for me to travel to England. I went there to study journalism. The Spanish people's fight against fascism inspired me to join the International Brigade. Somehow, I felt it was something like the struggle for Indian Independence. The Republicans were fighting for ideals like democracy and equality, which are dear to my heart. There were passionate discourses everywhere. Many people from other nations had already gone to Spain. I joined the British volunteers posing as a British citizen and headed for Spain."

CHAPTER 20

Huddar said, shrugging his shoulders, "Well, this is my story in brief. Why did you join?"

Henry narrated his story. Huddar whistled, "Then, life here is a far cry from what your life had been. You had not known a day's hardship before."

Henry smiled ruefully, "That, I confess, is true. Academics and sports now seem a leisurely life without parallel. But the war has taught me what real life is all about. It is pure hell."

Huddar said, "Yes, nothing to sing about. It also brings out the worst in people. But no matter how much people suffer, they can overcome all odds with hope in their breasts."

They left the café and shook hands. Henry said, "Goodbye until we meet again."

He did not know then how soon that would be and in what conditions.

Gandesa was a small quaint town resting on the river Ebro. Had it not been a place of action, it was a city of immense beauty with its rocky hillside and the tranquil river. Its first impression was one of quiet, where life went on at a steady pace in the redbrick houses covered with sloping tiled roofs. The church square dominated the town. It was famed for its wineries. However, its serenity was shattered as the city had become a war zone. The XV International Brigade had dug into the city. There were signs of fortification everywhere. Sandbags and machine gun turrets were erected beneath walls. In fact, wherever you went, there were sandbags. Barricades had been erected at various places. Men in uniform carrying guns were visible everywhere. A few columns of soldiers walked in the streets, their eyes alert. Most civilians stayed at home. They watched the situation peering through heavily curtained windows.

Sometimes, one saw someone dash out of the house to buy a few essential items and then dash in. The International Brigade seemed determined to hold the town. They were battle-ready. Word reached that the Nationalists were advancing towards Gandesa. It mainly comprised Mario Berti's CTV and Monasterio's Army Corps troops. As the army approached the outskirts of the town, firing intensified. Dead bodies were heaped. The number of wounded, too, was staggering.

Henry's task was to carry the wounded from the field to the nearest camp, from where other stretcher bearers would carry them for treatment. The International Brigade, mainly comprised of British troops, fought hard and valiantly. They tried their best to save the city. They could not save the city from falling but delayed its ultimate capitulation. The Nationalist troops met with unexpected hard resistance. Henry, too, felt that he was operating right in the midst of action; a bullet could get him anytime. His heart contracted at the sight of so many British soldiers lying dead. They would not receive any formal burial with their loved ones weeping around them. They would be buried right where they fell.

Then, it happened. It would bring another turn in Henry's life. Henry was busy in the field trying to take the wounded to safety. Bullets were flying all around him. The Nationalists were advancing and they were expected to take over the town at any minute. But the Republicans had decided not to give up. They fought back. Henry remembered Tennyson's Charge of the Light Brigade

Half a league, half a league,

Half a league onward,

All in the Valley of Death

Rode the six hundred.

"Forward, the Light Brigade!

Charge for the guns!" he said.

Into the Valley of Death

Rode the six hundred.

Except that the heroism displayed by the soldiers of the volunteers of the International Brigade would remain unsung without glory. It was sheer romanticism and idealism that drove them on. But sometimes, these lofty ideals were not enough. He recalled what the great novelist Albert Camus had said about the Spanish Civil War, 'It was in Spain that men learnt one can be right and still be beaten, that force can vanquish spirit, that there are times when courage is not its own reward. This, without doubt, explains why so many men worldwide regard the Spanish drama as a personal tragedy.'

A loudspeaker blared. A voice spoke, "You are surrounded from all sides. Surrender and prevent further bloodshed. There is no way you can escape. Our machine guns are trained on you." Almost everyone encircled realized that resistance would be futile. They threw up their hands in abject despair. Henry, who was tending to a wounded soldier, managed to tie him up and then shouted, "Medico, medico. Let us pass with the wounded."

He was not allowed. A soldier almost pushed him, saying, "Medico or not, you will be shot if you try to leave."

Something gave Henry courage, "I have not come here to fight. I am not a soldier. I am a stretcher bearer. This man I am carrying will die if he does not receive treatment. You are also a soldier. You should understand that no matter which side he is fighting for, a wounded soldier deserves help."

The soldier prodded him with his rifle butt. He said, "You are a prisoner of war. Just come with us."

"Why are you taking me when I am a medico?"

"You are working for the Republicans, aren't you?"

"Yes, I am."

A man who looked like being in a position of authority came forward. "Medico or not, you are our prisoner. March with the others. You will be clamped in jails."

There was nothing else Henry could say. He raised his hands. They were all taken on a single file with their hands raised and the guns pointed at them. From the corner of his eye, Henry spotted Huddar. He, too, was taken a prisoner, their fate uncertain.

A soldier said, "All of you will have to go for screening."

They nodded. Henry and the others were sent to a camp where a colonel interrogated them.

Henry was asked in broken English, "Where you from?"

"England"

The Colonel stared at him and then said with a dismissive stare, "One of the half-breeds there."

Henry had never felt so insulted in his life. Technically, he came from a mixed lineage, but no one had ever called him that to his face.

The Colonel asked again, "What are you doing in Spain?"

Henry said, his chin up, eyes defiant, "I am here to help the sick and the wounded – those who have suffered from the fascist onslaught."

Soon, the interrogation was over. They were all handcuffed. They were bundled into a truck with guns trained on them.

A soldier standing guard said, "No *hanky-panky* or monkey tricks. One movement from you and I will shoot."

Henry sat on the floor, squeezed between two other prisoners. The truck swayed from side to side as it travelled. Then, suddenly, it came to a jolting halt. They were at a station. Their handcuffs were removed, and they were taken out of the truck. The guns remained pointed at them. Henry could make out they were at a railway station. They were then huddled onboard a train to Burgos.

One of the British soldiers asked, "Where are you taking us?"

A soldier hit him with the end of the rifle butt and kicked him. He screamed. The soldier said, "Keep your mouth shut and mind your own business. Don't ask stupid questions. I could shoot you right here if I wanted to. So, do as you are told. A prisoner of war has no right to ask questions."

Henry squatted on the floor of the train, leaning on one side. He did not know where this new journey would take him. Every minute was uncertain.

CHAPTER 21

The train came to a halt and they were all commanded to get out. They were shepherded into another truck. The truck started and then, finally, they seemed to have arrived at their destination. The truck came to a screeching halt and they were bundled out. A huge grey monastery loomed in front of them. It was an old San Pedro de Cardeña monastery that had ceased operating in 1922. It was a three-storey building that had been built around an immense courtyard. A cathedral built in the Gothic style adjoined the monastery. It had now been reopened by the Nationalists and turned into a concentration camp. The main reason behind it was the large rooms which had the capacity to house 12,000 prisoners. They were taken inside. After a cursory examination and questioning by a sergeant, the members of the International Brigade, who were called internationals, were separated from the Spanish prisoners. No work was allotted to the prisoners of war belonging to the International Brigade. They were stripped of their clothing and given a set of clothes to wear. These were hardly adequate to keep away the late spring chill, especially at night. Henry was allotted a stay in a large hall along with several others. There were no open windows. The only ventilator in the room was heavily barred. It was extremely stuffy. The room was bare of any furniture, not even beds. Henry looked around. There seemed to be too many people housed in this single room. He tried to see if Huddar was one of them. He was not.

The man standing next to him spoke, "I am Leo from the British regiment."

Henry accepted his hand in a firm grasp. "I am Henry. I worked as a stretcher bearer."

"Well, good to have someone with a medical background besides me. You see my feet are swollen and my limbs ache like mad."

Henry said, "I am actually not qualified. I received hardly any training. Just gave first aid. Nothing much. When I was taken, I lost my first aid kit. They would have taken it away anyway."

Leo gave a faint smile. His face was contorted with agony. Henry said, "I will ask the guards if any treatment is available in this place. There should be a medical care centre or mini hospital. I have heard that most prisons have them. So many of our soldiers are wounded. They deserve treatment."

Henry went outside and asked a guard in Spanish, "My friend is sick. He needs help. Is there anywhere I can take him?"

Three to four guards were standing. One of them said, "Ask your friend to step outside. I will take him."

Leo stepped outside and when he returned, he said, "There is a Health Centre. There is a doc there too. But it is pretty useless. The only medicine available was aspirin. They gave me just one tablet."

Henry said, appalled but in a resigned voice, "They call themselves a health centre and there is nothing available. Don't they know that half the people here require help as they are wounded in war or very sick? But a tablet of aspirin is better than nothing."

"Yes. But where do we sleep? There are no beds."

Henry, his face hard, said, "On the stone floor, I guess. If we continue living in such overcrowded rooms, we are done for. Most of us will die of sickness. They can save their bullets. They won't have to shoot us."

Leo looked startled, "Do you think this is what they intend to do?"

Henry nodded grimly, "Most probably."

Leo suddenly said, "Do you want to die?"

Henry shook his head, "Strangely, no. I want to live. Life has much to offer yet."

"What do you want to do if we escape scot-free?"

Henry looked doubtfully at Leo and said, "Go back home and to college, I guess. But I feel it will not be the same. The war here has changed me." Henry kept quiet.

Leo said, "Me too. I have not planned what I'll do when I go back."

Supper was served. The food was very poor, just bread and a watery preparation of beans. When darkness descended, they were handed out rolls of thin, rugged-looking blankets. The unlucky ones got tattered ones too.

The guard said, "Mass at six. You should be up by then."

Someone asked, "Where will we go?'

The guard said in a harsh tone, "Don't ask questions. You will find out tomorrow."

Leo whispered to Henry, "So, we are expected to sleep on the stone floor. We shall face cold nights."

Henry thought he would never sleep, but strangely enough, he fell asleep the moment he covered himself with the blanket. Perhaps, it was because he was dead tired.

His eyes opened at the crack of dawn. Although it was still dark, a faint light was visible through the barred window. He got up and simply ran his fingers through his hair. There was no place he could wash. They were heralded into the nearby chapel where a brown-robed priest presided in the best Catholic traditions. Guards stood with sticks in their hands. When they were expected to kneel and if they did not do it properly, blows fell on them, making them cry out in pain.

Henry discovered that prisoners from the International Brigade did not have to work. The Spaniards who had been captured were forced to work in iron mines where harsh treatment was meted out to them if they slipped up in their duties.

Minutes passed into hours, and hours into days. Many fell sick and suffered from dysentery. The room smelt of stinking waste. It was difficult not to puke. A set of fresh clothes was not always available. The food was inferior. Every morning, they would be given a loaf of bread required to last throughout the day. The bread was often stale and sometimes, filled with maggots. Lunch and supper consisted of watery beans. A few days, if they were fortunate, they would be served kidney beans - but there was hardly any variation. At times, a piece of rubbery stale pork was given. Morning drill was compulsory. Even the sick and exhausted prisoners were forced to participate in it. If they made mistakes, they were severely disciplined. Although the morning drill exposed them to the outside air it left a bitter taste in their mouths.

What most prisoners looked forward to was the day they were allowed to go to the river to wash themselves. It was great to inhale fresh air and go outdoors for a brief time. Walking on the occasional grassy patches surrounded by ancient trees felt rejuvenating. Most men did not talk among themselves. They were just glad to be able to walk freely, even if it was momentary. The wash in the river felt as near to heaven as they could get, even though the water was cold at times, making them shiver. It was exhilarating to feel clean again after a life in confinement and squalor for days.

There were many attempts to convert the prisoners to fascism. Just a few days after being confined, the prisoners were asked to go to the lawn area. A thin priest stood there, preaching fascism and saying that they had been led astray. The priest denounced democracy and communism as evil and fascism as good for the soul. After that, the Commandant of the camp appeared along with several officers. He asked the prisoners to sing the fascist anthem *Cara al Sol* ('Face to the Sun'). Everyone was expected to join in. If you did not, you were severely beaten. Henry, like most others, did join. After all, the great bard Shakespeare had said, "The better part of valour is discretion," in *Henry IV*. At length, the ceremony came to an end. A Nationalist military officer roared, 'España', which evoked a response from the Spanish prisoners, '*Una*!' Then, there were shouts of Franco. The prisoners were forced to give the fascist salute. If they refused, they were beaten black and blue.

Most of the time, the members of the International Brigade remained confined in the rooms. They had nothing to do except talk.

One day, Leo told Henry, "I wonder what they will do to us. Maybe execute us. Our countries are doing nothing to help us."

Henry answered, "None of us here know the answers. All I realise is that we have to somehow pass our time here."

Another fair-haired man with an ugly gash on his forehead called Martin said, "Let us play a game of chess."

With a puzzled frown, Henry said, "But we don't have a chess board or pieces."

Martin smiled, "Our imprisonment has heightened our creativity. I know a few things from what goes on in the other hall. They have torn different shapes of dry bread into chess pieces and drawn a board on the floor." He smiled, "It helps to kill time."

Henry gave him an incredulous look, "The height of man's ingenuity. But let us play."

The chess board was drawn, and the game began. There were other activities to engage their time. The English-speaking prisoners started a newspaper called the *Daily*

News. The prisoners, including Henry, wrote their feelings and pasted them on the walls. These were removed when the guards arrived but not before others had read them.

While these activities helped to relieve boredom, they led a troubled life. Illness and death plagued them. Many inmates died from festering wounds, while others died of unsanitary conditions resulting in disease. Henry was extremely shocked and hit to the core when he saw a blond sixteen-year-old boy being carried out. He had died of dysentery. Every other day, bodies continued to be carried out. Beatings by guards continued, which left them half-crippled.

CHAPTER 22

The worst problem was lice. They crawled all over and got into your pants, making you wriggle in a frenzy. They had got so used to it that if one of them saw lice crawling off a fellow prisoner's shoulder, he killed it. Physically drained and exhausted, they were also subjected to mental torture, including fascist propaganda. Leaflets were distributed in different languages glorifying the fascists and setting up a communist phobia. Extreme false claims were flying about as propaganda stating that a communist takeover of Spain seemed imminent and this was the main reason Franco came into the scene to save his own countrymen. A movie, "*Prisioneros de Guerra*," was made, portraying life in prison as a glorified ideal. The prisoners who claimed to be members of the International Brigade said they were lured by 'Soviet gold.' They were being rehabilitated under the leadership of Franco.

Besides putting up with the usual hardships, the prisoners were interrogated by the Gestapo. These were more severe with German prisoners belonging to the International Brigade. The Gestapo man sat with a ledger in his hand behind a desk. One by one, each prisoner was called. Henry, too was called. After the preliminary questions were over and his identity established, the Gestapo officer called his assistant. "Take out the callipers and measure." To his horror, Henry was forced to lie down and stripped while the assistant measured the length and breadth of his skull, nose and other features. He noted the scars the prisoner had and listed them down. Even the colour of his skin and his body type was noted. Henry felt utterly humiliated. This was not the end.

Two German sociologists visited the prison. One of them said, "We are only trying to help you. Just fill in the questionnaire."

A huge bundle of papers was handed over to each prisoner. Henry gasped when he was presented with his bunch. He was flabbergasted by the detailed questionnaire presented to him. Who had thought of this poppycock and who would take the trouble in reading what he had written? There were around two hundred questions. Most questions were related to morality. Henry found that he was required to fill in details about his family background, including its history, any criminal activity history, drunkenness, illegitimacy, his position in society, religious and political affiliation and even his sexual preferences. The questionnaire also included details of his military history, education levels, and diseases, including mental illness. A theory floated that the root cause for Republican support was the criminal mentality of the prisoners rather than political ideals. They needed redemption.

One day, Henry found Leo sobbing. Henry asked, "What is wrong?"

Leo wiped his eyes and said, "Bad news from home."

Henry looked concerned. He lay his hand on his shoulder in silent sympathy.

Leo spoke again after another fit of sobbing, “It is my old man. He is gone.”

“What happened?”

“Cardiac arrest. That’s what the doctor said. My mother wrote. The poor dear must be a broken woman. They had thirty-five years of married life. Their love was seen to be believed. What will my mother do? I don’t know.”

“Do you have any siblings? Are they around to comfort your mother?”

“I am the only son. I have two sisters. I guess they are around.”

He burst into another round of sobbing. “They have laid him to rest and I wasn’t there. The funeral too is over with everyone in the village attending except me. He was a popular man. The information reached me late. Here I am, rotting in prison, unsure if I will live or die. I can’t even go to see her. I don’t know how she is bearing her grief.”

Henry simply said, “It is hard. Can’t you ask the jail commandant for special permission to go home?”

Leo smiled weakly, “You don’t believe it is a real possibility, do you? He would just tell me to go to hell and probably have me thrashed as well.”

Henry nodded. He did not say anything. What could he say? Leo continued, “My father did not want me to join. He felt I should stay back in the village and do something useful. He called me and said, 'Leo, the trouble with you is that you are hot-headed. If you want to help others, do something in the village. There is a lot of scope. Do something for your country. Idealism and romantic notions don't work in real life. Things are never as they seem. Why punish yourself for a cause which has nothing to do with your own? You will suffer and no one will be grateful for your contribution. They will not even know about it. My son, listen to reason. Stay here. The Republicans can take care of themselves.'"

Leo shook his head, "I did not listen to him then. I was all for stopping the Nazis. I don't think we have succeeded. Franco's regime will start sooner than later."

Henry answered quietly, "My father was against it too. Still, I do not have any regrets. I feel that even if I die tomorrow, I will die for the best cause in the world – fighting for freedom. I feel a man is born to live with choices. The Franco regime will not give us a choice. Even if I am free, I feel I may fight for another cause later. Of course, that's still in the future. Who knows, I may change my mind."

After his conversation with Leo, Henry reflected that he had been selfish in choosing to fight for the Republican cause. He could have stayed back for his parents. That evening, he wrote to his parents. He simply stated that he was well. He was not allowed to write more – just give a message.

However, life in jail did have a bright spot or so. The prisoners were allowed to attend classes. The San Pedro Institute of Higher Learning organized such classes. The language classes were very popular. Henry, too enrolled on a Spanish language class. It was always good to brush up on what you know. There were economics, history, mathematics, the arts and philosophy classes. In one of the classes, Henry met Huddar.

Both shook hands, and after the customary how are yous were exchanged, Huddar whispered, "They are likely to shoot us. This is the dope I have got."

Henry said, "They should have done it at once. I don't know their purpose of keeping us alive."

"Yes. But we have almost lost the war. Gandesa has fallen and the news I have heard is that they are closing in on Madrid. It may not be long."

Henry said bitterly, "This war will only embolden Hitler. He will be hungry for more pastures. I hope and pray he tastes defeat soon."

The guards who saw them chatting shouted, "Away to your rooms. Do you want to be flogged?"

Henry felt the fever coming on. His limbs ached and his heartbeat was fast. He lay in one corner of the stone floor shivering uncontrollably. His head ached so much that he felt it would burst. He cried out in sheer agony. He felt surely this was the end. He remembered the other time he had a fever. At that time, there was a warm bed with Rosa at his side. Now, he was all alone, wanting to just slip into the darkness and face oblivion.

CHAPTER 23

Henry lay in a stupor, not knowing what was happening around him. He thought he couldn't care less. All his focus was on his body. His heart ran fast, as if taking part in a sprinting race, his body burned, and he felt too weak to get up. The stone floor felt like it was made of ice, but he could not leave it. Whenever he tried, hands pulled him back. Leo's and Martin's faces took shape in the shadowy recesses of his mind. One of them said he was not sure who, "Do not get up. You are too weak." Someone using gentle hands put a cold compress on his forehead. It felt a bit better. Someone else lifted him by his shoulder and gave him water or made him eat those watery beans with a piece of pork thrown in – a rarity. Someone else said, "You have to eat if you want to get well."

Henry grimaced but obeyed. He then said, "I am a dying man. Why are you taking so much trouble to save me?"

It was Leo's gruff voice that answered, "Nonsense. You cannot leave us in this way. If we face a firing squad, we face it together."

Henry gave a weak smile. He was made to swallow a tablet, maybe aspirin. Over the next two days, his fever abated. He felt less weak and was actually able to sit up and notice his surroundings. Leo and Martin were constantly by his side, looking after him. No one could have nursed him better.

Slowly, Henry's strength came back. He told Martin, "You and Leo have been my ministering angels; it is you who have pulled me from the jaws of death. I was a goner otherwise."

Leo said gruffly, "Don't thank us. We have a bond closer than friends. We are brother prisoners knowing we would die. We are just helping each other bear the ordeal better."

Martin said, "I know you would do the same for us."

Henry's eyes filled with tears. He quickly wiped them away with the back of his hand. He said in a voice choked with emotions, "Whatever happens to us, we are in it together. The prison has given me lifelong friends." He hugged both Martin and Leo together.

Slowly, Henry's strength recovered. One day, Martin had a visitor. It was his sweetheart who was allowed a brief visit. One of the guards said, "We are not inhuman, you know; we understand emotions."

Martin went off alone. His eyes were shining and his face had turned beetroot red. He returned after an hour. His eyes swam with tears. Leo and Henry simply hugged him. All Martin could blabber was, "This may be the last time I have met her. We have no future together. I may be shot tomorrow, for all I know. I told her to go her own way."

Henry placed a consoling hand on his shoulder. Martin managed to say, "It's hard. Terribly hard. I would have said the same thing if she were my wife."

Henry and Leo looked on, shocked. Suddenly, Henry thought of Rosa. In a way, he was glad that she was not with him. There would be one lesser person to mourn for him if anything happened to him.

Would he die? He did not know. All he knew was that he still wanted to live despite his torment.

Martin brought him another piece of news, "I have something that interests you."

Henry raised his eyebrows, "The famous Indian leader Jawaharlal Nehru is in Spain."

Henry exclaimed, "Good for him. How did you know?"

He said, "I have got quite pally with a guard. He handed me a newspaper. I couldn't smuggle it here. Otherwise, I could have shown you. I managed to read it from the front page to the last."

Henry smiled, "It's like unearthing a treasure. Tell me about it. Second-hand information is better."

"Nehru came to Barcelona. He was accompanied by his daughter, Indira. She is supposed to be a beauty."

Henry said eagerly, "I have seen her."

"Ah, then you would know better if the reports on her beauty are true. But Nehru has extended support. Krishna Menon was also there. He is, if reports believe, very close to Nehru. He has not minced words in condemning Chamberlain's appeasement politics. The newspaper states that Nehru was impressed by the courage and determination shown by the Republicans despite hardship and want. Nehru stayed there for five days and every night, the bombs fell. He felt that the Spanish people displayed exemplary courage in doing something worthwhile; Nehru got around. He is a generous man and has a human touch. He met not only important politicians, including the President and foreign minister of the Republican government, but also leaders of trade unions and communist leaders. He even visited the battlefront and met officers of the Republican army. A few members of the International Brigade were lucky to meet him."

Henry said, "Then, he must have also promoted India's cause."

Martin smiled, "Ah, yes, he did. But I don't know if there were any takers. The Republican government was, of course, very happy to have a leader of his stature visit their country. But their primary concern was to aid the Republican cause through propaganda. They put their best foot forward. The Republican government hosted two receptions in his honour where he spoke eloquently and compared India's fight for freedom with the struggle for freedom and democracy in Spain. He spoke against fascism and the menace that Hitler represented."

"Ah, any fresh news on that front?"

"Plenty. Some from newspapers and others from fellow prisoners. One of them manages to listen to the radio in the Guards' room."

"Hitler is going strong, very strong. All guns blazing. You know that he has gobbled up Austria; now it is the turn of Czechoslovakia. He has demanded Sudetenland. His excuse was that ethnic Germans were under attack. He got the support of a minor pro-Nazi group led by Konrad Henlein.

It was Hitler's voice speaking through Konrad demanding political autonomy for Sudetenland. Hitler thundered in Berlin and demanded an autonomous Sudetenland or war from the Czechoslovakian leader Benes."

"He is likely to get it."

"He has already won. I hate to say it, but your British Prime minister had a major role to play."

Henry muttered, "Neville Chamberlain has always had knee-jerk reactions to Hitler."

"This time, it has crossed all limits and he thinks he has done some great diplomacy and played peacemaker. This September, he has had three meetings with Hitler. Other leaders, including Mussolini and Edouard Daladier of France, are involved. The result of these meetings was the Munich Agreement. The papers are full of it and nothing else is discussed. All of them literally forced Czechoslovakia to concede Sudetenland to Germany. Germany agreed not to ask for more territory from that unfortunate country. The Munich Agreement put a legal stamp on it. Unfortunately, even the people of Britain welcomed the move. Chamberlain received a tumultuous welcome back home. He had brought peace. Czechoslovakia was sacrificed to avert war. On the very first day of October, German troops rolled into Sudetenland. I doubt if war has been really averted. It will come sooner than later."

Henry nodded grimly, "I doubt Hitler will rest content now that he has tasted success. I wonder which country he will eye next."

No one knew the answer to that question.

CHAPTER 24

It was now growing colder. At times, bitter winds blew. The prisoners rubbed their hands and feet and tried to keep warm. Unfortunately, it was Martin who fell sick. One day, Henry noticed Martin was coughing on and off. He did not pay attention as Martin appeared to be his usual self. When Henry expressed concern, Martin laughed, "It is just a cough. Everyone gets them. It will go away." He patted Henry's arm.

But it did not go away. It persisted and got worse, and it was a moist cough. He was spitting out phlegm. Henry insisted that he see the prison doctor. Martin refused. "I am just down with a common cough and cold. What would the doctor do anyway? He hardly has medicines."

A couple of days later, Henry found Martin lying listlessly in one corner. Dawn had broken, and they were called for mass. Henry shook Martin away. His entire body was burning, and he was shivering violently. Henry spoke to the guards, "My friend here is ill, very ill. A prison doctor needs to see him."

The guard looked at him sympathetically, "I will try to fetch him after Mass. The authorities are strict about attending Mass. Your friend can meanwhile lie in his room."

Henry hurried to his hall after Mass. Martin was still lying listlessly. He was breathing slightly heavily. Henry again spoke to the guard, "Have you spoken to the doctor?"

The guard scratched his head and said, "I did go, but the doctor said he was busy and it would take time. Too many prison inmates are sick. Some of the guards too."

Henry muttered under his breath, "He had better hurry up."

Leo, who was beside Henry, suggested giving cold compresses. He had torn a strip from one of his pyjamas and made a cold compress with available water. A couple of hours passed by, but the doctor did not come. Henry and Leo waited for the doctor, their eyes towards the door. When Henry again questioned the guard, he sounded impatient. "I have told the doc. I am sure he will come. It takes time. Just three doctors are attending to too many patients. Get back to your cell, and do not bother me again."

Henry went back seething in anger. Will his friend never get help? It was late evening when the doctor arrived. He examined Martin with a stethoscope. His face was grim. He said, "Your friend has pneumonia. I will try to shift him to the healthcare centre. Meanwhile, send the guard to the centre. I will hand some medicines to him."

As the doctor was going out of the door, Henry followed him. He said, "Doctor, will my friend recover?"

The doctor answered after a pause, "It is difficult to predict. It is a pretty severe case. I will do my best, but we have meagre resources. With the war raging, medicines are in short supply."

Henry did not say anything. He only hoped and prayed that his friend would get timely help and get back to being his old self. Henry and Leo sat at night with Martin. The guard had handed them a few medicines with a message from the doctor. The guard said, "The doctor told me to tell you that this is all I have got."

Shifting him to the prison healthcare centre took two long days. By that time, Martin was much worse. The intensity of his coughing increased and his fever showed no signs of breaking. The doctor was grim. His only comment was, "He would be lucky if he pulled through."

Henry pleaded, "Can't he be moved to a better hospital?"

The doctor shrugged his shoulder and said, "I will try my best. I will write to the prison authorities and seek permission. But let me tell you frankly that I feel that there is very little hope of them agreeing. I have taken this route often but without success."

"Please take care of him," Henry pleaded.

The doctor said, "You may be prisoners, but don't worry. Your friend here will receive the best treatment possible. I am a doctor by profession. I do not care if my patient is a prisoner or a high official. I do my best for them. I will make one allowance. You can visit the patient every evening."

The fever raged and wracked. Martin was very weak. While attending to Martin, he got news about Huddar from another fellow attendant to a patient.

"There is a pretty dark fellow from India or Iraq. I am not sure which who calls himself John Smith."

Henry said. "I know him. Is he well?"

"Doing fine. He has gained a reputation in palmistry among prisoners, of course. I don't know how much of it is correct. Some of it seems to be. He told a fellow prisoner that he had two brothers and two sisters, which was absolutely right. He told another that he had married twice, and again, he hit the bull's eye. He has made many predictions and answered a lot of questions. I, too, had my palm read. I asked him only one question – whether I had a long life. He said yes, I will live to a ripe old age and die in my bed. His fortune-telling was extremely consoling. It meant I would get out of prison; that's what matters to me at present."

Henry smiled, "That's the paramount thought in all our minds." Henry's thoughts once again veered towards Martin. Would he be able to survive?

The question was difficult to answer. Hardly any progress was made. Martin seemed to worsen. One day, he said to Henry, "I feel it is better to die the death of a soldier even if you are executed by a firing squad. Death is immediate. You hardly feel anything. It is better than this lingering death in a prison cell."

Henry said vehemently, "Don't talk of dying. You will be well. Think of it."

Martin gave him a sad smile. "That's not true. I feel that I am a dying man. Do inform my girl and family when I am dead."

Henry was almost choked with emotion. Martin patted his hand. "Don't take it hard. You have been a good friend.

If I come face to face with God, I will ask Him to send you home to England."

Henry could not hold back his tears. He averted his face, got up and went outside, the tears falling thick and fast. This was the last time Martin was able to talk to him lucidly. He slipped into delirium. The Spanish doctor was true to his word. He did his best to procure whatever medicines he could but knew he was fighting a losing battle. Then, after a week, he called Henry and said, "I am afraid your friend is dead. He died just an hour before. He was unconscious, so you can console yourself with the thought that his last moments were relatively peaceful."

He is dead. The words had a ring of finality about it. Although Henry had dreaded hearing the words, he knew it could happen. Martin had been very sick. Yet, he was shocked with disbelief. All he could do was hug Leo and cry. He let his tears flow while images of Martin kept floating in his mind. Martin teaching them how to play chess, the sound of his laughter, his red face when he met his sweetheart, his general awareness about what was happening around him, and the way he animatedly discussed the political situation – a budding life was sniffed out. Martin was only 23; his whole life had stretched before him.

They buried him in the compound of the prison. Leo and Henry were allowed to attend the service. There was no stone edifice. He would be among the many who would have to be content to rest on this piece of the earth among the myriad of others brought here daily.

CHAPTER 25

Almost a month had passed since Martin's death. The cold had also increased. Most prisoners shivered in what were almost rags. It was tough to get through the daily drill. The water in the river where they were taken to bathe was freezing. All Henry could enjoy was the brief glimpse he had of the outside world and a little bit of exercise.

He reflected that in his jail tenure, many foreigners had visited them. One of them was William Carney of the New York Times. He seemed a fascist to the core and had very little sympathy for the members of the International Brigade. He had gone home and written an article about what he felt was an ideal prison. All the prisoners gained were cigarettes given by the members of the press. Lady Austen Chamberlain was perhaps the most important visitor. She was the sister-in-law of Prime Minister Neville Chamberlain. The prisoners were handed over new shoes and a set of clothes in preparation for her visit. However, many of them refused to give her the fascist salute, and they were beaten black and blue.

Henry also reflected though the prisoners of the International Brigades seemed a friendly lot, deprivation and hard living conditions made them quarrelsome. Fistfights usually broke out over food. Henry remembered that once a pan of sardines was going to be served. The smell of the fish made everyone scramble to be first in the queue. This resulted in a fistfight between two burly members. Leo and Henry tried to play peacemaker and managed to separate them. They were all scared of the beatings with the heavy stick. A new sergeant had come who ordered beatings at the flimsiest of excuses. It could be a sloppy salute to Franco or any indiscipline. Once, its weight fell on Henry, too, for not saluting properly. He was taken to a room where the blows fell hard and fast. Writhing on the floor, he was kicked around like a ball by other sadistic guards. At that time, as he lay on the floor, he felt that he would never be able to get up again. It took more than a week for Henry to recover. His skin was black and blue with bruises. He found it difficult to lie down or even sit. The pain was unbearable whenever he tried to lie down.

Meanwhile, although Henry had no mood for it, the prisoners were preparing for a concert at Christmas. They were staging a play. Some were preparing folk songs. Henry, although still grieving for Martin, was forced to help them out. He did not participate in the play but helped out with the backstage arrangements and promptings. Soon, 1938 would come to an end. He hoped nothing untoward would happen.

Something did happen. It was, again, a life-changing event. In fact, there would be no life at all. It was a cold day in mid-November. Icy winds were blowing, biting into the skin. It heralded a freezing winter. Henry hugged himself as every breath seemed like cigarette smoke bellowing up in the air. The sergeant came into the room and called out a few names. Henry, to his surprise, found his name being called. Leo's was too. In a crisp, commanding voice, the sergeant said, "All British prisoners are to report in the courtyard."

Henry and Leo talked about it with the other prisoners. "What could it be?"

Leo said, "I haven't a clue. Whatever it is, it cannot be anything good. A more severe punishment, perhaps."

Henry sighed, "Sometimes, I feel that anything, even a quick death is preferable to the torture we are undergoing here. Everything is so dirty, even the state of the loos. Cleaning them is a job worse than scavengers."

They were supposed to report to the courtyard in the afternoon. The moment they entered the courtyard, they understood why they had been called. Machine Guns were lined up at one end. Henry and Leo looked at each other. They knew the purpose of being called. They had been brought here to be shot. Henry thought, '*So, this is the end.*' The possibility of death had always been there from the moment he stepped into Spain. His duties often took him right into the heart of the action, where a bullet might get him at any time. There had always been the prospect of danger and death. But that was different. With his body already wasted, he would be shot like a criminal for no crime. Henry had often thought about death in Spain. Death was a constant companion in Spain. He knew what he was getting into when he came, and so did Robert. It was the end of the serene life he had led so far – a life of comparative ease and leisure which seemed a far cry now. But death by execution was something Henry had not considered in his wildest dreams. Strangely, when he was now face to face with death, it was not Rosa he thought about. It was his parents. How would they receive this news? It would devastate them. Henry meant everything to his mother and she would be a broken woman. His father, for all his lectures, loved him intensely. Henry yearned to see their faces again, kiss the earth of English soil, hear the nightingale sing and the thrush chirp, and simply loll in the hills of the English countryside and taste his mother's cooking. Home had never seemed sweeter. Yet, although he felt many emotions of sadness and nostalgia, the one experience he did not experience was regret. He did not regret his decision to come to Spain and participate in the war. He had met so many people, some of them celebrities, some ordinary human beings. He had made many friends – all of them bound by danger. At that time, his thoughts went to Miguel. He wondered how he was faring. So, this was death. He could console himself that it would be a quick one. There will not be much suffering.

Leo suggested, "We have to be resigned to our fate."

Henry thought he could not be resigned. He felt another surge of intense emotion – it was the desire to live. There was so much to do. Now that he knew his fate, all fear had disappeared. He spoke boldly, "What is my crime that I will be shot like a dog?"

The guard answered, "We have orders."

The gunners took up their positions, their hands on the trigger. Henry cast a quick glance at the other prisoners. They were standing with their eyes shut. Henry thought it would be over soon, and he braced himself to take the bullet. He thought he would do it with his eyes open. He wanted to have a last glimpse of the world he had inhabited – the sky, the sun, the clouds and even the prison walls. Death had come and he wanted to face it.

Then, the miracle happened.

A man came running to the courtyard waving a sheaf of papers, screaming, "Stop. Don't shoot. These prisoners are to be released."

The gunners let go of the triggers and their hands fell on their side.

A man's voice, maybe a commander, asked, "Why?"

The man said, "The British authorities are here. They want all British prisoners to be set free in lieu of them being exchanged for the Nationalists in our custody. They have the requisite documents. There is no room for error. The orders are very clear."

Above the loud voices, Henry heard Leo's voice shouting in exhilaration, "We are free."

Henry slumped down, drained of all energy. By a miracle of God, he had been saved in the very nick of time. At that time, he did not know how it all transpired. He did not care since the end result was so exhilarating. If the order came one second late, his body would have lain slumped to the ground and later, buried in one of the mass graves. He shook his head. He would soon be free – free to go home.

EPILOGUE

Henry sat on the train to Paris along with Leo. From the window, he watched the Spanish countryside whizz past him. The beauty of the countryside had almost gone. One could catch a few glimpses of it at times. A few cottages stood intact with their garden. The sparkle of the Mediterranean remained, though spoiled by menacing warships. The grass was still green in patches but most had dried and withered. In many places, the earth itself was singed. Everywhere the eyes went one saw only ruins of once proud buildings with debris piled. He said a silent goodbye to the country he was unlikely to see again. In a few hours, he would reach Paris. From Paris, he would catch the London train and then head straight for home.

Henry's father had written a very emotional letter welcoming his son back home when he heard the news. Henry was ready to comply. As he sat on the train, Henry reflected on his last few days. There had been a whirlwind of activity. He had been curious to know how his final freedom came about. Henry had come to know that the British officials had arrived almost at that very moment at the monastery with the release papers. They went straight to the Commandant and learnt to their shock that the prisoners were about to be shot. The official immediately ordered a halt to the proceedings and threatened that even if one man was hurt, the prisoner exchange would not occur. A harassed Spanish official had run out at top speed and fortunately, reached the place before even a bullet was fired.

Henry's last day in the San Pedro prison was memorable in more than one way. He recalled being surprised when they told him a visitor was waiting for him at the reception area. He wondered who it was. As he approached, he came face to face with Rosa. She had come with Bert. A wedding ring graced her finger. She held out both her hands and he grasped them in a warm clasp. After the preliminary how are yous were exchanged, Rosa explained that she had heard about his capture and imprisonment from the officer at his base camp in Madrid. She had come to inform him about her marriage.

Bert shook his hand and said, "Rosa considered you a close friend. She felt that you care about our well-being and wanted to tell you the news. We could not inform you about our wedding as it was a small affair with just families, considering the times we live in." Bert sounded almost apologetic.

Henry said, "I can understand. I was probably in jail then."

Henry then smiled at Rosa, "I can see that you both are glowing with happiness. I wish you luck."

His words were genuine from his heart. That feeling of loss was gone. He had gradually come to accept the reality that she had never loved him. Her heart belonged to someone else. After his days in prison, he realized that there are many things worse than pining for what could have been but never was.

Rosa said, "I am so glad to hear that you have been released and are finally going home. You have done such a lot for my country."

Henry smiled ruefully, "I don't know if it has been of any use. Madrid will fall any day. Franco will rule. His revenge will be terrible. Take care of yourselves."

Rosa gave him a warm smile and said with intensity, "Never again say it has been of no use. You have done what very few human beings achieve in a lifetime. You have unselfishly served others without self-interest. You have served in this war without caring for fame, money or position. I think that is the epitome of humanity."

Henry almost choked, but it gave him a sense of satisfaction. He had not failed. He sat on the train, thinking how he got there. After his release, he was taken to a temporary jail. There the facilities were better.

He heard that his friend, Huddar, had been released. It was a last-minute rescue. It was Leo who told him the story. "The friend you talked about, John Smith, an Iraqi who turned out to be an Indian."

Henry had laughed, "He was always an Indian; never went to Iraq in his life."

"True. I don't know how the story got around in the jail about him being an Iraqi. Anyway, he too is free. The story of his release is even more dramatic than ours. He too was marked to be shot. Few people knew about his origin. Another team of British officials visited our jail. Among them was a Colonel from British India. He immediately recognized John Smith as an Indian and hence, a British subject. By a strange coincidence, the Colonel was from Nagpur the city to which John Smith belonged. It was this Colonel who got him released."

This was a very welcome news.

Later, he received another heartening news. Henry came to know that Miguel was safe in Switzerland. He was working in a hospital there. The train chugged on. A sudden thought came into Henry's mind. '*Would he do it again if he got a chance?*' Strangely, despite all his sufferings, his answer was yes. He had been useful to other human beings who were also suffering. This thought alone boosted his morale. He was a changed man beginning a new journey. He did not know where this journey would take him.

www.ingramcontent.com/pod-product-compliance
Lightning Source LLC
LaVergne TN
LVHW041206150826
845673LV00001B/309

* 9 7 9 8 8 9 0 6 7 8 3 4 8 *